Storm

in

the

West

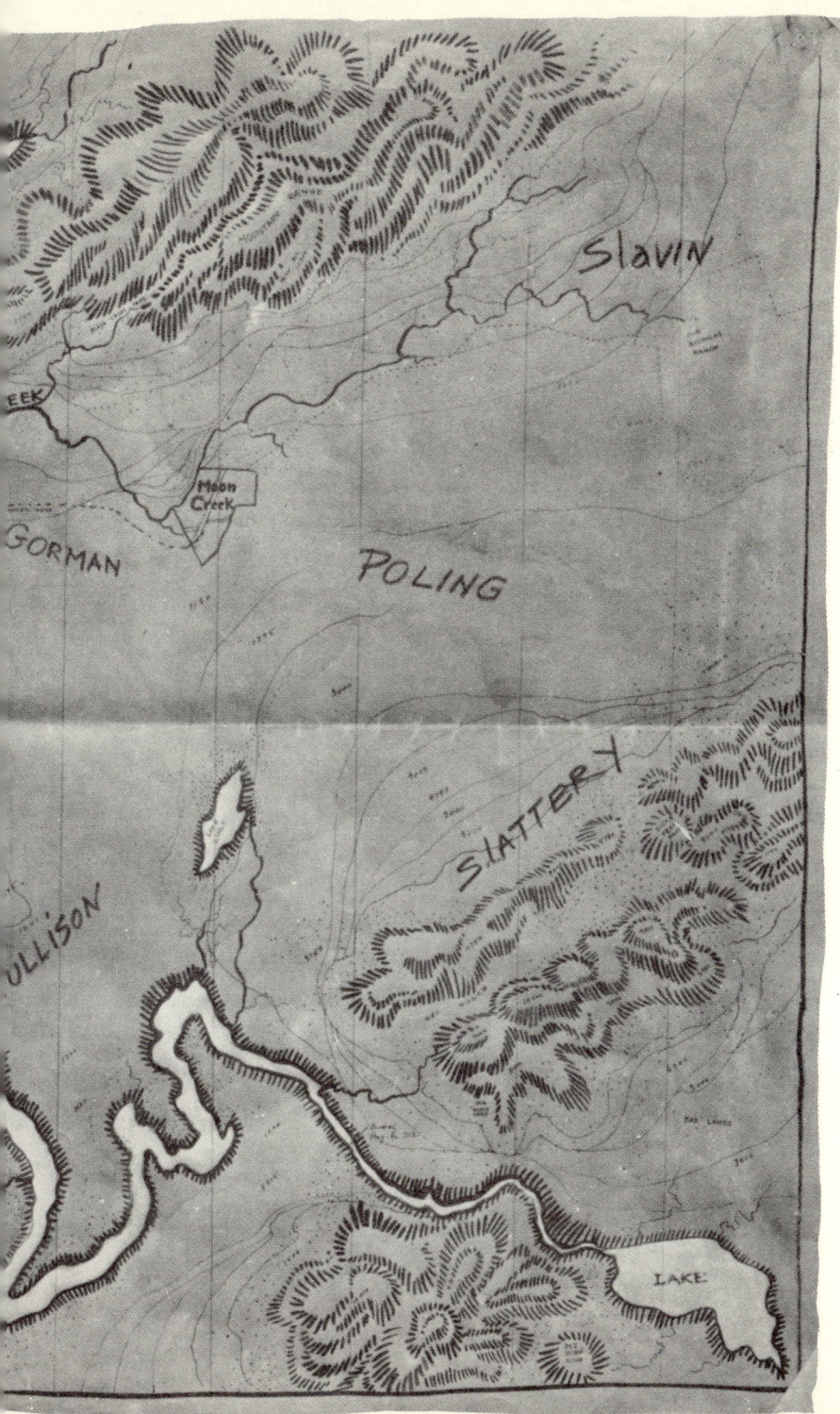

Storm

A SCARBOROUGH BOOK
STEIN AND DAY/*Publishers*/ New York

in the West

BY *Sinclair Lewis*

AND *Dore Schary*

WITH AN INTRODUCTION BY *Dore Schary*

ILLUSTRATIONS BY SOL BAER FIELDING

FIRST SCARBOROUGH BOOKS EDITION 1981

Storm in the West was originally published by Stein and Day/*Publishers* in hardcover.
Copyright © 1963 by Stein and Day, Incorporated
"Storm in the West" Copyright © 1963 by Metro-Goldwyn-Mayer, Inc.
Foreword, "Working with 'Red' Lewis" Copyright © 1963 by Dore Schary
Illustrations Copyright © 1963 by Stein and Day, Incorporated

Library of Congress Catalog Card No. 63-13228
ISBN 0-8128-6079-9

All rights reserved. No part of this book may be reproduced in any form or by any mechanical means, including mimeograph and tape recorder, without permission in writing from the publisher, except by a reviewer who may quote brief passages in a review to be printed in a magazine or newspaper.

Designed by David Miller
Printed in the United States of America

STEIN AND DAY/*Publishers*
Scarborough House
Briarcliff Manor, N.Y. 10510

Storm

in

the

West

AT WORK WITH "RED" LEWIS

A Foreword by Dore Schary

In the spring of 1943 I had an idea for a motion picture. At that time I was employed by Metro-Goldwyn-Mayer and had just resigned my post as executive head of their low budget film department to concentrate on writing and producing pictures that would be my personal productions.

On June 14th of that year I sent Mr. Floyd Hendrickson, the head of M-G-M's legal department, the following enigmatic memo:

Dear Floyd:

I am sending to you a sealed envelope with an original idea enclosed. This is an idea for a motion picture which I have discussed with

Mr. Lichtman, Mr. McGuinness, Mr. Weingarten, Mr. Fadiman and Mr. Beecher.

We are now searching for a proper setup and a distinguished writer to do the screenplay.

It is what we believe to be a very important idea and a very tricky one and we do not want too many people to know what the notion is, but yet we want a certain protection on it. That accounts for this rather secretive and confidential method of registration, which was suggested by Mr. Beecher.

The copy that you have in the attached envelope is the only copy. I have the original in my desk and there are no others. Does all this make sense to you?

On the same day, Mr. Hendrickson replied:

This will acknowledge receipt of your memorandum enclosing sealed envelope *Thunder over the Plains* by Dore Schary. I will keep this envelope in my files unopened until such time as we can announce the story.

Within a week after this exchange the title of the story had been switched to *Storm in the West*. I had also made contact with Sinclair Lewis via telephone, and he had agreed to work with me and was on his way to the coast.

I had read most of what Sinclair Lewis had written, and he seemed an ideal choice to collaborate with me on the story I wanted to tell. He knew the West, his ear was accurate, and his political orientation seemed to match mine. In addition to all that, he was enormously enthused about the idea of *Storm in the West*. He told me that while he had sworn never to forgive M-G-M for not having made his novel *It Can't Happen Here* into a film, he would forswear his oath "made in the blood of a New England rooster."

The nature of show business is one part enthusiasm, one part skill, one part experience, one part luck. The auguries for *Storm in the West* seemed good. We had enthusiasm, Red's skill, my experience, and luck seemed to be running our way.

What I had dreamed up as a film was an allegory. I wrote out my notions in a memo dated June 9, 1943, parts of which follow:

"The purpose of this picture is to tell the story of the world history of the last ten years in terms of what we might call a realistic allegory. The story itself, in terms of nations and personalities of our contemporary life, presents itself in dramatic symbols. . . . The story bears repetition and must be told so that if nothing else, people can be told again the methods of Naziism and how best we can by collective security hang on, not desperately, but triumphantly to what we know is the way of life we want to live. . . . The villains are the Fascist and Nazi villains, and the heroes are the democratic heroes. But the background is not Europe and modern America, the time is not 1933 to 1943.

"The locale is the American west of 1880. Our cast of characters . . . are all American frontiersmen, hard, salty, tough, colloquial men. The villains are realistic, the heroes are realistic, men of flesh and body and soul.

"The story line involving these characters parallels the rise to power of Hitler and Mussolini..."

Then in sketchy outline I duplicated the events of the last ten years in allegorical terms. It was full of the timidity, the doubts, the confusion, and the double-dealing that led up to the attack on Poland by the Nazis in September, 1939. It seemed to make dramatic and pictorial sense. I concluded my initial notes with a reminder and warning to myself as the producer:

"The one big point behind the entire production must be the fact that no one connected with it should be concerned too much with the symbols that they stand for. They must be concerned with the people and the characters that have been created for them. The direction must be related to a western motion picture, not a picture of significance. The whole thing must be done so that when it is finished and shown, a person who had never heard of Hitler and the second world war could look at it and enjoy it for what it is."

The arrival of Sinclair Lewis in Hollywood to work on *Storm in the West* provided good publicity for the proposed picture. Red was always a good talker, and his pungent interviews did us no harm. I had never met Red, did not know his working habits or idiosyncrasies. I learned fast enough. Red liked to work businessmen's hours. He came to my home at ten o'clock in the morning, spent an hour or so talking about California, its climate, its wondrously gifted girls, its lack of good newspapers, and then off we'd go into pinwheels of work.

At this time Red was on the wagon. He was a chain smoker, and his heavily brown-stained fingers were never free of a cigarette. He was not particular about what happened to the ashes (they wound up on the carpet, on his trousers, shirts, or jackets), and he consumed them with insatiable deep inhalations. As he talked he was forever surrounded by a blue haze of smoke that softened the outlines of his head and partially hid the scars on his face.

While Red was not drinking liquor his body required oceans of liquids—all of it iced coffee. On his arrival the first morning, he asked for a large glass of iced coffee—"a long glass, lots of sugar and some cream, thank you." The first glass was drained in a few minutes, and when the glass had been refilled and emptied again in a short time I suggested we get a pitcherful and keep it next to Mr. Lewis. He thought that was a dandy idea.

Each day that we worked the pitcher was near Red's right arm, and each day he consumed a staggering amount of the coffee, watered down by ice and flavored by sugar and cream. As he talked and drank and smoked, the screenplay of *Storm in the West* came into being. Red would excuse himself an extraordinary number of times to make his way to the toilet, and often when he reappeared he would say, "Standing in your miserable, small convenience, I had an idea—"

His early ideas had to do with names. He told me he could not work constructively on the plot lines or scenes until the names seemed to belong to the characters. So for a few days we labored over the names, discarding hundreds but eventually agreeing on our Cast of Characters:

The United States was Ulysses Saunders; Adolf Hitler was Arnold Hygatt; Goering became Gerrett; Goebbels became Gribbles; Mussolini remained Mullison; Chamberlain was Chambers; Red preferred that Saunders' daughter be named Pearl, instead of Priscilla. I had some serious reservations about that, but Red was adamant and I agreed. France would be Franson; Poland was

Poling; Germany was Gorman; the Junker clique were to be under the leadership of (who else?) Al Yunker; Norway was Norton; Quisling was Quist; Stalin became Slavin and Churchill, Chancel.

Finally the names satisfied both of us, and we went to work on the script. First we outlined the structure of our screenplay, occasionally taking time out to detail a scene that intrigued us. We dictated this treatment, and it went smoothly. Lewis had a boyish enthusiasm and would chortle at some particular line or thought that pleased him. All during this time the pitchers of iced coffee were at hand wherever we worked—in my study, outdoors under the wisteria arbor, or those rare times when we worked at the studio.

He was pencil-lean and would fold like a carpenter's ruler whenever he sat down. When we began work on the screenplay, Red would collapse into a chair, then straighten up and push out of it onto his feet whenever a happy idea struck him. He was a pacer when he worked, and so am I. As we talked our way into and out of scenes we would pass each other many times, and often Red would greet me as we crossed paths with "Morning, Brother Schary" or "Didn't I see you at the Turkey Shoot last Saturday?" or "There's talk, Brother Schary, you been servicing the Widow Greene."

As the script progressed, Red became even more enthusiastic, and his optimism sparked me.

We had a first draft ready by the middle of August, far ahead of our work schedule. We began to prune, revise, and rewrite. But I knew that no matter how well we worked, no matter how well-conceived our screenplay might be, we would still have to find a director whose eye would see the film as we planned it. The most difficult achievement in the making of a film is for the writer, director, producer, and the heads of all departments concerned to have a common image of what the film will look like when it is finished. Often a writer abandons his literary style, knowing very well that there is no point in explicit descriptions; once the script leaves his hands, the producer and then the director move in and take over.

Circumstances have changed for the better in recent years, and writers remain closer to their work. There are writer-directors, producer-writers, and even director-producer-writers, and the reason for their proliferation stems from the old frustration of not being able to control the original image of their work.

Since I was going to be the producer on *Storm in the West,* I felt I would be able to translate the conception that Red and I shared. I had a list of directors to choose from—Victor Fleming, Bill Van Dyke, William Wellman, and one or two new directors we had developed in our small-budget unit, Fred Zinneman or Jules Dassin.

This comment about imagery is not tangential to the story of *Storm in the West* since so much of it depended on precise images—so precise that at some future time, after the picture was finished, all of us who had anything to do with it could be able to view it and say in unison, "That's exactly the way I wanted it to look."

As a beginning step toward achieving the image we wanted, I assigned Sol Baer Fielding, a capable artist then working at the studio as an associate producer, to draw pictures for us that would illustrate to the reader exactly what we had in mind. Those pictures are reproduced in this volume.

Meanwhile, day by day, Red and I labored at our screenplay and discussed the imagery, dialogue, and scene structure.

Red became part of our household. He knew our children and liked them, and they in turn liked him. He was extremely fond of my wife, Miriam, and he addressed her with various titles—Madam Schary, Lady of the Manor, Frau Schary, and (once in a while) Miriam. One day he arrived with a gift for Miriam: a miniature cactus garden. It was about two feet long and had a small rock garden formation all in scale with the small cacti.

If there is anything Miriam detests (and there certainly is), she detests the desert and its "blooms" most of all. But she oh'ed and ah'ed for Red, and we found a place for it on the patio, and each day Red would go out to take a look at his flourishing gift.

But what Red didn't know was that some of his miniature cacti had an illness. As they died off one by one they were replaced early each morning by our florist, who assumed we had all gone sentimentally mad over our miniature garden.

But Miriam felt Red would be hurt and embarrassed if he knew the plants were dying; so she kept up the deception until the day Red entrained for New York. Then she disposed of it, and our florist bill decreased proportionally.

The days sped by—we breezed through July and August, and the script was finished and mimeographed and in that strange double talk of mimeograph departments was labeled "Temporary-Complete" and sent to various executives and department heads.

Red and I said farewell to each other early in September, and on the 14th of that month he wrote to tell me of a long weekend trip he had made to Boston, Salem, Marblehead, and Rockport. He told me that New England was his favorite part of the world.

At the Studio the debate had started. The executives were divided in their opinions. Half were delighted with the script, the other half dismayed.

At that time, decisions were made by what we called "M-G-M's College of Cardinals." The executives decided by majority vote what stories the studio would make into films. While L. B. Mayer could, as he often did, force his will on the board, he would, if he were unsure, go along with with the majority.

Storm in the West now found itself the center of an intramural struggle. I appeared in front of the board and fought for the right to make the picture; but the pressure against the script was heavy, and Mr. Mayer ducked the issue by saying he would let Mr. Nicholas Schenck, the President of the Company, make the final decision. Weeks had gone by during which time I had heard from Red, who was waiting impatiently for the good word.

In October, Lillie Messinger, who was a close adviser to Mr. Mayer on story and script matters, left for New York to discuss the project with Mr. Schenck and Howard Dietz.

I sweated out the days that followed, but finally, on October 20th, I wired Miss Messinger to ask whether she had conferred with Mr. Schenck. Receiving no answer to my first inquiry, I wired on October 22nd a cryptic "Well?" Five days later I wired "Boy, Girl, Twins or Tumor?"

It was a tumor. Miss Messinger wired me that she thought Mr. Mayer had brought me up to date with a telephone conversation he had had with

Mr. Schenck, during which they had decided to abandon the script.

That telegram took me into Mr. Mayer's office, and I learned then that some executives felt there was "too much politics" in the script and that since we were fighting a war against Naziism why should we keep talking about it? There had been complaints about the use of the sickle and hammer to identify Slavin as Stalin. This complaint was so irritating and so ridiculous I lost my patience. I argued, but it was useless. The decision was made. Mr. Mayer suggested I forget the matter and go to something else.

I said I wanted to go to *somewhere* else—I wanted to quit. I had a few years left on my contract and so I needed a legal release before I was free to leave. Mr. Mayer said he would let me know in a few days whether they would let me go.

A few days later, I was told by Mr. Mannix, Mr. Mayer's chief aide at the time, that permission had been granted and that I was a free agent.

On November 4th I wrote Red what had happened. On the 14th he answered that he was shocked. Well, that made two of us.

A few weeks later I had located myself with David O. Selznick, who wanted me to make some films for him under the banner of his subsidiary company called Vanguard.

I tried to buy *Storm in the West,* but it was

not for sale. Neither was it for sale some years later when I was at R.K.O.

By the time I got back to M-G-M, in 1948, I was so involved in discussions over current films in work that I never even thought about *Storm in the West*.

The screenplay you are about to read is as it was written except that technical terms have been translated into narrative story telling. There were notes Red and I had made for rewrite and some changes, but we never got to them.

In 1947 when I visited Red in New York we talked about the script, and Red pointed out that in 1943 we had been prophetic in predicting the way Hitler and Mussolini died. Red suggested that if things got bad for both of us we might open a tea-leaf reading salon.

When you have been defeated, as I was in trying to get *Storm in the West* produced, you always search for a slight glimmer of glory on which to rest your weary heart. Bad notices on a play make you seek out those people who saw the play and said, "I *liked* it." If your book gets good notices but doesn't sell, you can always reread the praises that were sung. My experience with *Storm in the West* brought me something I cherished: friendship with "Red" Lewis.

Years later when I stood before his grave in Florence I remembered the sad and haunted look on his face; it was there when he laughed or played or worked. It was the look of a man who lived with a secret pain that he would reveal to no one. I remembered with affection the swirl of smoke that always covered him, the sickly cacti, the warm California days, the parlor games that delighted him so, and of course I remembered the iced coffee.

It is night in a small midwestern town. Inside the simple one-room jail, a wall of iron bars splits the room into two, one the cell proper, for the prisoners, and the other a combination entry room and jailer's watch place. In the cell, a prisoner sits on a bench, his head in his hands. The jailer consults his watch, then gets up from his desk near the door leading into the jail.

He fusses with his key chain as he talks to the prisoner: "All right, Hygatt, your thirty days are up. Kinda fussy about these things—you were brought in thirty days ago at eight o'clock at night, and it's now thirty seconds to eight o'clock at night." He opens the door. "Come on, get goin'."

The prisoner rises. He is about thirty-five years old. A thatch of black hair tumbles down over his left brow. He wears a short black moustache. He is dressed very simply, dark pants, boots, brown shirt, and a black frontier hat which he now picks up from the rough bunk on which he has slept. He is the sort of man, whom, if you met casually, you would think was rather inoffensive and mild until you looked deep into his eyes. His physical movements are wiry and quick.

Jailer: "Come out here, and I'll give you your gear."

Hygatt, the prisoner, walks out to the jailer's desk. The jailer sits behind his desk and opens the drawers. He takes out a large canvas sack, throws it on the desk. Out tumbles some stuff, including a small wallet. The jailer opens it and looks in. "You had ten dollars. Count it."

Hygatt takes the wallet and puts it in his pocket.

Jailer: "A gun belt and a .44. . . ." He looks at Hygatt. "That yours?"

Hygatt nods.

Jailer, as Hygatt readies himself: "Let me tell you something, young fellow. I've seen a lot of bad men in my day, like the Daltons and Jesse James and Al Yunker. They all started out the same way, like you, thirty days in the hoosegow and then a longer time, and they get harder to handle. But finally they're put away where they can't do nobody no harm no more, and that's where you're headin' for, a little space six feet under the ground and a tombstone that says, 'Here lies Arnold Hygatt.' Take my advice, get yourself a decent job, and change the company you keep."

The jailer, as he talks to him, is not astute enough to see the fire in Hygatt's face. Hygatt doesn't say a word. Just then the outer door opens and in comes the deputy sheriff, preceded by two villainous-looking men. One of them is a big, powerful, heavy-muscled fellow. This is Gerrett.

The other, Gribbles, is a slim, short, wry-faced fellow who limps from an old injury to his right knee.

The deputy carries on his left arm the gun belts and guns of the two new prisoners. He closes the door behind him, calling to the jailer: "Couple of new customers, Pop. They're to be held on a murder charge."

Jailer: "Business is kind of lively."

Gerrett looks off in the direction of Hygatt: "Hello, Hygatt."

Hygatt looks up and turns in the direction of Gerrett. He waves a little salute to Gerrett.

Gribbles: "Too bad you're leavin'."

Gerrett: "There's no place like a jail for really getting acquainted."

Jailer, standing up: "Stop chewin' the rag and get in there." He motions to Hygatt: "Get goin'."

Hygatt walks toward the door. He passes Gerrett and Gribbles who are headed toward the cell. The deputy also passes Hygatt. Hygatt suddenly turns, takes out his revolver, and smashes the butt of it onto the head of the deputy—twice in rapid and vicious succession.

Hygatt, quickly, to the jailer: "All right, Pop, up!"

The jailer lifts his hands, and as he does so Gerrett, with his powerful right arm, smashes the side of the jailer's neck. The jailer sinks unconscious to the floor.

Gribbles looks disinterestedly at the jailer: "Probably killed him."

Gerrett, just as disinterestedly: "I wouldn't wonder."

Hygatt: "Get your guns."

Quickly Gerrett and Gribbles get their belts from the unconscious deputy. As they start out Gerrett kicks the deputy's head for good measure.

Hygatt, with a little smile to the two men: "What are we waitin' for?"

They come out of the jail, closing the door behind them, and stand expectantly waiting for trouble.

Gerrett, his voice low: "Where to?"

Hygatt: "West."

Gribbles: "What's West?"

Hygatt: "Let's find out."

The three of them start down the street.

A Western Territory—July 4, 1875

The little village of Homeville, a frontier cow town in the middle of the Western plains, has one main street with a number of small dwellings on both sides. The population of the town is about two hundred. It is now early morning. This being July, it is a hot day. Some people are moving up and down the main street. Two riders are heading toward the town.

One of them, Chuck Slattery, a young, handsome man of about twenty-five, rides a sorrel. He is a husky, well-muscled fellow, amiable and intelligent. Chuck gives the impression of being a working cow rancher and not a fellow fresh from a rodeo.

On his right rides Peterson, known as Pete. Peterson is a thin, wiry man about sixty years old with a mop of very fine white hair. Peterson rides a short cow pony. He wears overalls with a black, semi-Prince Albert coat over them and a broad-brimmed black frontier hat.

Chuck and Peterson, as they walk their horses, look toward the town, aware of the sound of the firecrackers and excitement. Chuck looks over at Peterson and smiles.

Peterson: "The Lord loveth a cheerful noise, and what's good enough for the Lord is good enough for me."

Chuck: "The town sure does look like a holiday."

By now they have reached the edge of the bridge which crosses the river bordering the town. The horses' hoofs, clumping across the log bridge, make a good solid sound. The river bed, this time of year, is almost dry. As they walk their horses across the bridge Chuck looks off to his left and smiles proudly at a small schoolhouse built of flimsy planks. It has a steeple not over three feet high in which is a brassy-voiced little bell. A flagpole in the front yard, simply a shaved sapling, proudly holds an American flag on which are thirty-eight stars. In front of the school is a large open space, and grouped in this area today are a number of crude wooden tables and benches.

Peterson: "Chuck, I can remember back to when that flag only had twenty-six stars."

Chuck nods. As they proceed up the street, the first building they pass is a combination barber shop and meat and salt-fish store. Appropriate signs proclaim this to the population. This store, like most of the others in Homeville, commemorates the Fourth of July by displays of bunting and American flags.

Outside the barber shop a couple of men wave at Chuck and Peterson, and Peterson waves a salute back at them.

One of the men, calling to Chuck: "Hey, you! Chuck Slattery! Come on in and get yourself prettied up."

Chuck, with a smile as he calls back: "Ain't done you much good, Red." He proceeds up the street.

The next place they pass is a blacksmith shop. The blacksmith, dressed for a celebration, is closing the door to his barn. Outside the blacksmith shop are one or two pieces of farm machinery that need repair.

Next Chuck and Peterson pass the stage office. It is closed for the day, but on the porch sits a chubby man, who waves a friendly greeting at Chuck. A sign on the building reads:

**OVERLAND STAGE
AND FREIGHT COMPANY**
Fast Freight Connecting with
Railroads to: Salt Lake City,
Denver, Cheyenne, Omaha.

As they proceed up the street the next building houses the Blackjack Saloon, a respectable establishment, not too typical of the frontier saloon. This establishment has a nice display of bunting and has a homemade pasteboard shield with the bunting draped about it.

Just as Chuck and Peterson come by the Blackjack, two boys, aged about thirteen, throw a string of firecrackers under the swinging doors. As the firecrackers rattle off, the kids hightail it, and Holly, the bartender, comes storming into view, kicking the firecrackers out of the saloon.

Holly shouts after the kids, but not too angrily: "If I get my hands on you long-eared, spavin-brained—" His speech trails off and he looks up in the direction of Chuck. "Seein' today's a holiday, Chuck, you can have one on the house." He smiles at Pete. "And there's a bottle of pop for you, Reverend."

Chuck and Peterson wave in acknowledgement.

Peterson: "We'll drop by for that later, Brother Holly."

As they pass the saloon, they come to the Sheriff's office, identified by a sign which reads:

Sheriff's Office
Ned Chambers, Sheriff

As Chuck and Peterson move past the Sheriff's office, and just as they approach the office of *The Blizzard,* the town's newspaper, they hear very faintly the voices of a group of children singing "Oh, Columbia, the Gem of the Ocean." Their voices are accompanied by a reedy, wheezy parlor organ.

The sign on the Blizzard office reads:

THE HOMEVILLE BLIZZARD
Published Twice a Month—Often
Only Newspaper in Masterson County
Walter Chancel—*Ed. and Prop.*

In front of the Blizzard office, Wally Chancel, the editor and proprietor, is stacking up some special copies of the paper. Chancel is a stocky, powerful, middle-aged man. A cigar is clamped between his firm jaws.

Chuck, calling out: "Wally, you oughta put 'Deputy Sheriff' underneath that 'Editor and Proprietor' sign. Ain't you wearin' your new star?"

Chancel, showing the star underneath his vest: "Don't believe in mixin' business and pleasure." With a grin: "And I ain't sayin' which is which."

Now Chuck and Pete are in front of Ulysses Saunders' general store, an unusually large and well-kept establishment. In front of it is a hitching rail for horses and a large covered porch. Two show windows display clothes and equipment of the period. Above this porch can be seen the windows of the second floor. They are adorned with rather prim lace curtains. A large sign in front of the porch says:

THE HOMEVILLE BOSTON STORE
Ulysses Saunders, *Proprietor*

An American flag hangs from a pole out of one of the upper windows.

On the opposite side of the street from Saunders' store are a harness, saddle, and boot store, some other dwellings, and another saloon.

Chuck and Peterson get off their horses in front of the general store, walk up the steps, and continue on into the store.

This is a well-stocked establishment. The shelves are packed with every variety of goods that anyone in the vicinity might want, all neatly arranged on shelves. On the left is a long counter, and at the far end is a higher section of counter which Ulysses Saunders reserves for his bookkeeping.

Saunders is at the far end of the counter, and as Chuck and Peterson enter, Chuck calls out: "Happy birthday, Mr. Saunders."

Peterson: "Greetings, Brother Saunders."

Saunders looks up to acknowledge the greeting. He is a tall, well set-up man, a Vermont type of American, about fifty-five. He is a genial businessman in control of his mind at all times, but he gives the impression of being qualified to put up a good fight if he ever gets into one. He wears a short chin beard that is grizzled and sprinkled with gray. His ample mop of hair is also streaked with gray. He wears much the same store clothes that he might have worn back in New England, clean, heavy trousers, worn over high black shoes, a woolen vest which is open at the moment and across which hangs a heavy watch chain with an elk's tooth and a bear's claw dangling from it. A cartridge belt with a heavy .44 in the holster lies on the counter next to him. It looks as though it has had some use.

Saunders is not wearing his coat, and there is a spendid view of his starched, round, linen cuffs which are detachable and fastened to the sleeves with old-fashioned spring clips. The shirt has a starched white bosom, and he wears a high Gladstone collar but no tie. He is a figure of rustic dignity and prosperity.

In back of Saunders and facing the counter is a very large, heavy, solid-looking safe, which is open. Perched on the safe is a large, stuffed bald eagle. It's a good job of taxidermy, and the eagle, its claws around the ball of the standard, must have been a hell of a bird when it was alive. Its head faces the door, and as Saunders looks up quizzically there is a momentary resemblance between him and the eagle.

Saunders, looking up: "Hi, Chuck—Reverend."

Peterson: "Birthdays ain't altogether a pleasure once you get past fifty, Brother Saunders."

Saunders: "Most men my age would like to forget about their birthdays but not me. I can still outlift the huskiest man around here."

Chuck: "You sure can."

They hear the children singing "Columbia, the Gem of the Ocean." Saunders looks up in the direction of the singing. So does Chuck.

Saunders, shaking his head: "How long does it take those kids to learn a tune?"

The singing goes sour and stops. Chuck smiles at this, then speaks to Saunders: "Say, the stage bring in a package for me yesterday?"

Peterson, eagerly: "And for me?"

Saunders nods, reaches back in the safe and brings out two packages, one of them a small flat package and the other a small jewel box. He hands the flat package to Chuck and the other one to Peterson.

Saunders: "There you be."

Peterson starts to unwrap his package, but Chuck holds his and then hands it back to Saunders.

Chuck: "Just kind of a little birthday remembrance, Mr. Saunders."

Saunders, as he takes the package: "Mighty nice of you, Chuck, mighty."

Chuck: "Go on, open it up."

Saunders opens the package and reveals a rather fancy bow tie already made up with an elastic band.

Saunders: "Say that's mighty good looking." He takes it out and tries to snap it on.

Chuck: "Let me give you a hand with that."

Now his hands join Saunders, and between the two of them they finally get it snapped on, but it's awry. Chuck now pushes it around in front and tries to straighten it up and despite his big hands, does a fairly good job.

Peterson has opened his package and has been looking at it. He holds the little box before him.

Peterson murmurs softly: "Look at it, Brother Saunders."

Saunders and Chuck look at the box which Peterson holds out for them with his left hand. Peterson removes his hat with his right hand. He has an awed look on his face. Chuck and Saunders examine the object without touching it.

Chuck: "What is it, Pete?"

Pete: "It's a Roman coin of the time of our Lord. The ad in *The Weekly* said it was the only one extant." Explaining to the two of them: "That means the only one still around."

Saunders and Chuck look at the small box in which there is a heavy Roman coin, recently polished.

Saunders: "Nice. What'd they soak you?"

Peterson: "It don't matter. It don't matter." He looks at the coin.

Peterson, softly: "His fingers might have touched it when He drove the money changers out of the temple." He closes his eyes a half second, visualizing the picture in his mind. He closes the box, puts it away carefully in his coat pocket. "I'll see you later, Chuck. I want to show the coin to the editor. Maybe he'll write something about it."

He walks out. Chuck and Saunders watch him go.

Saunders, closing the account book he has been working on and putting it into the safe: "Poor Peterson, I reckon there are a million of them coins 'extant.'"

Chuck: "A fellow's lucky when he can believe in somethin'." Then with a little shrug: "I'll be mighty glad when Peterson gets that little chapel built out at my place. I think he was more cut out for preachin' than for cow-handlin'."

Just at this moment the voices of the children start up again. Saunders looks up at the ceiling once more as he locks the safe. He takes his coat and walks from behind the counter toward the front of the store.

Saunders: "Chuck, that daughter of mine is a persistent girl. She's made up her mind that those kids are goin' to sing 'Columbia the Gem of the Ocean.'" He shakes his head. "And by Jerusalem, they're goin' to learn it if it kills them and me—and her."

Chuck, smiling: "Is she that way about everything, Mr. Saunders?"

Saunders: "Pretty nigh. If you mean about her going back east to Illinois, she's going, Chuck—in the fall."

Chuck, with a smile: "I'm kind of a persistent fellow myself." Then with a broader smile: "And fall's two months away."

Saunders nods and claps Chuck on the back. By this time they have left the front of the store, and they walk out, Saunders locking the front door behind him.

Saunders finishes locking the store, goes down the steps with Chuck and walks to the side. He and Chuck start up the covered staircase at one side of the building. At the head of the steps Saunders opens the door, and he and Chuck walk into the Saunders' living room. The entrance into this room from the back steps is at the rear of the room. Facing the street are two windows, decorated with starched lace curtains and flowers between them. Against the wall is a stiff, upholstered black walnut sofa. The chairs are comfortable, not too formal. The cane-seated rocking chair is beside a table on which Saunders' pipe and tobacco jar rest. Other items of furniture include a "patent rocker," an ornate but worn armchair, some assorted prairie wildflowers in hand-painted and home-painted jars and tin cans. At the right of the room is an ornate parlor organ above which a sign reads, *"He Will Lead Us."*

At the organ sits Pearl Saunders, a pretty and healthy-looking girl in a calico dress. Though she seems strong enough to ride a cow pony for hours, she is really a village type rather than a fantastic buckskin-clad Annie Oakley.

Grouped in front of the organ, facing Pearl, are ten children of from five to twelve years old. Six of these children are girls wearing festive Fourth of July costumes of cheesecloth with red, white, and blue sashes, homemade affairs and not very elegant. The four boys are dressed in their Sunday clothes, but they also have important-looking sashes draped from their right shoulders to their waists. One of the boys, the smallest, wears a high hat which is decorated with a band of white stars.

As Chuck and Saunders enter, the children reach the third or fourth line of the song "Columbia, the Gem of the Ocean." One high falsetto voice ruins the rendition. The children turn in disgust to look at the traitor.

One of the children: "Joey, you done it again."

Pearl looks up and sees Chuck and Saunders. She waves a little greeting at them.

Pearl, to the children: "Well, children, I think that's about enough." She gets up from the organ. "Now I want all of you to be at the schoolyard at three o'clock sharp, and take good care of those costumes and see that nothing happens to them."

A Girl, the oldest of the group: "Miss Saunders, what do we do this afternoon? Do we just go right on singing no matter what happens?"

Pearl nods: "No matter what."

One of the Boys: "Last one down's a squaw Indian."

They all storm toward the door. As they smash out of the room, practically pushing Chuck and Saunders to one side, the children acknowledge the presence of the two men by shouting.

Children: "Hi Mr. Saunders. 'Scuse me. Hello Chuck."

The door slams, and the people inside hear the children storming down the wooden steps, then a firecracker going off, and finally the voices of the children yelling as they run down the street.

Saunders listens patiently, and as the sound of the children dies out he looks at Pearl.

Saunders, sardonically: "Bless their little hearts."

Pearl steps close to her father and looks at the tie. "Where did you ever get that?"

Saunders, indicating Chuck: "Birthday present."

Pearl, to Chuck: "That's very fashionable, Chuck—and congratulations to you. I have been trying to get him to wear a tie for five years."

Chuck: "The only reason I gave him a present was to have him on my side." He smiles. "We decided that you're not going east."

Pearl smiles without answer, crosses over, and takes out a small package. She crosses back to her father and hands the package to him.

Pearl: "And here's my present."

As Saunders takes the package and starts to open it, Pearl looks over at Chuck: "This is going to keep him on my side. I am going east, Chuck."

Chuck: "Pearl, you got as much education as any person'd need."

By now Saunders has opened the package: "Well look at that."

Chuck and Pearl walk over to Saunders. He has taken the present from the box. It is a black silk watch fob. On it in red, white, and blue silk stitching are a crude American eagle, a star, and Saunders' initials, U.S.

Pearl: "Do you really like it, Dad?"

Saunders: "It's handsome."

Pearl: "Happy Birthday and many more."

Saunders puts his arms around her and holds her close. Then he releases her and immediately begins to transfer his watch from the chain to the fob.

Saunders, as he does this: "Golly, Pearl, that's handsome. A thing like this in Chicago would run you fourteen or fifteen dollars—cash."

He now has the watch on the fob, and he looks at it, tries it out in his pocket, and puts the heavy chain down on top of the bureau.

At that moment there is the sound of a heavy, slow pounding.

Saunders: "Now what are those kids up to?"

The pounding continues.

Chuck: "Have to be a mighty husky kid to make that much racket."

Saunders walks toward the front window and looks down. From the window he can see a large Conestoga wagon pulled by a team of husky black horses. Sitting on the front seat, shaded partly from his view, is a woman, Mrs. Slavin. Grouped around the wagon are seven horses, and on the horses sit seven young men ranging in age from fourteen to twenty-six, all sons of Mr. and Mrs. Joel Slavin. These young men, dressed in work clothes and riding boots, are well-armed. They look as though they have covered quite some territory. They are dark, husky lads, and they all have some sort of family characteristic which makes them obviously brothers. They give the appearance of a hard-working family. Strung out and back of the wagon are four or five cattle and a bull.

Saunders, yelling down: "Yah?"

The seven boys look up at Saunders, and Mrs. Slavin puts her head out from under the wagon, looks up for a moment, and then slumps back. Nobody says anything.

Saunders, again: "Yah? What's up?"

Now, from under the porch, comes Joel Slavin. He walks down the steps, then turns to look up at Saunders. Slavin is a powerfully built man with a shock of black hair and a heavy black moustache. He wears a rough homespun suit. His pants are tucked into high plain boots that reach almost to his knee. He wears a simple gray flannel shirt, open at the neck. When he comes from under the porch and looks up at Saunders, he is wiping the brim of his black frontier hat with a large red bandana.

Slavin: "Gotta have supplies."

Saunders: "Fourth of July, closed till five o'clock."

Slavin: "I gotta be a long way from here at five."

Saunders looks back in the direction of Chuck and Pearl, then looks down again at Slavin.

Saunders: "Be right down."

Saunders turns away from the window, starts to the door.

Pearl: "You go along with Dad, Chuck. I must get into my best dress."

Chuck, as he walks after Saunders, looking at Pearl: "The blue one?"

Pearl, with a smile: "How did you know I had a blue dress?"

Chuck: "I also know you got a red dress, but my favorite one is the plum colored dress with sort of white stuff around the collar and kind of—" He makes a gesture indicating a wide skirt, but doesn't find any words to fit.

Pearl: "Oh, you mean the one that also has the—" She indicates puffed shoulders but doesn't say anything.

Chuck nods his head. "That's the one."

Pearl: "Well, if that's your favorite—I'll wear it." Then mock-politely: "Mr. Slattery."

Chuck, with a little bow: "Thank you, ma'am." He follows Saunders out of the room.

Slavin's boys are still mounted on their horses as Saunders comes around from the stairway and clumps up the steps. Slavin is waiting for him under the porch near the front door. He is a completely relaxed man, but he gives the impression that he could move into action in an instant. He is laconic and appears as pliable as a steel rail.

Saunders, taking out his key and opening the door, makes conversation: "Come a long way, haven't you?"

Slavin nods.

Saunders: "Too bad you're in such a hurry. Might enjoy the celebration here with us."

By this time the door is open, and Saunders walks in with Slavin in back of him. Chuck now walks up the steps and follows Slavin in. Saunders turns and faces Slavin.

Saunders: "Well, what'll it be?"

Slavin takes out a long list and hands it to Saunders. Saunders looks at it. Slavin looks at Chuck.

Chuck, pleasantly: "Hi."

Slavin nods. Meanwhile, Saunders looks at the slip Slavin has given him. One side of this sheet is printed:

SPECIAL AUCTION
September 14, 1874

Farm Implements and Stock
Waycross, Georgia

All Supplies, Equipment, Feed and Stock
The Slavin Farm

Slavin has seen Saunders read the printing, and as Saunders looks up: "What I want's on the other side."

Saunders: "You from Georgia?"

Slavin nods. Saunders now gets down to business and looks at the list.

Saunders: "That's a healthy order." Then, looking at Chuck: "Give me a hand, Chuck."

Slavin, calling out: "Boys."

The oldest boy, Alec, beckons to the others, but he calls to the youngest one, Tom: "Keep an eye, Tom."

He again beckons to the others, and they walk in, all six of them.

Saunders and Chuck look up with surprised amusement as the six young men clump into the store.

Saunders, to Slavin: "Private army?"

Slavin, by way of identification: "My sons."

Saunders gets down to business, indicating what the boys are to take out. He constantly refers to the list as he does this.

Saunders: "There's the barrel of flour, over there the bacon—two sides."

Two of the boys take the barrel of flour and start to roll it.

Slavin: "George."

George, who is one of the boys at the flour barrel, looks up a little shamefacedly and just beckons to the other boy, and the two of them pick up the barrel of flour and walk out with it.

Chuck has seated himself on a cracker-barrel and is watching all the activity, amused at this very unusual family.

In the street next to Saunders' store, Ned Chambers comes out of the sheriff's office. He is a tall, angular-looking man, thinner than Saunders and older. He wears a heavy shoebrush moustache and has a large hooked nose. The general impression is of a pleasant and good principled man but a weak one. His identifying sheriff's badge is on his vest.

He closes the door behind him and then goes next door to the Blizzard office by the simple means of climbing over a short railing that is between the two offices. He opens the door and walks into the Blizzard office. This is a plain, crude, newspaper office typical of the West. Chancel with his coat off is setting type in a form. His cigar is clamped between his jaws, and near him is a bottle of liquor and a glass. As Chambers enters Chancel acknowledges his entrance.

Chancel: "Hi, Ned."

Chambers walks over to Chancel. In back of Chancel on the wall can be seen some of his printing handiwork. There are some announcements about dances and sales and a framed copy of the first edition of the Blizzard, and featured so that we can see it instantly is a copy of a handbill which reads:

WANTED FOR MURDER—AL YUNKER

There is a picture of Al Yunker, a completely bald man. His left eye is covered by a black, round patch, and above his left eye, running into the black patch, is a jagged scar that disappears under the patch and then appears again below the patch and continues running into the cheek. Underneath the picture are the words:

REWARD—DEAD OR ALIVE—$500

Chambers: "What you settin' up?"

Chancel: "I'm runnin' out some handbills for 'Lysses." He points to the liquor. "Help yourself."

Chambers, shaking his head: "I been comin' in here for nine years, and you been offerin' me a drink for nine years, and I been sayin' no—for nine years."

Chancel puts some liquor in the glass and drinks down a good slug. He puts the glass down.

Chancel, as he does this: "And for nine years it's given me an excuse to take a drink myself."

Chambers, pointing to Yunker's poster: "I was talkin' to Belger this mornin', and he told me that on one of his trips to Omaha he thought he seen Al Yunker."

Chancel, turning and looking at the picture: "Was he sure?"

Chambers: "No. He thought he got a look at him in a saloon, but he figured he didn't want to make sure because, like he said, he figured the chance of getting a five hundred dollar reward wasn't worth getting killed."

Chancel turns away, picks up some waste, and starts wiping his hands.

Chambers: "Let's pick up 'Lysses."

Chancel nods, drops the waste, and slips into his coat. As Chambers crosses to the door, Chancel pours another hooker for himself.

Chancel, lifting the glass: "Your health, Ned." He drains the glass.

Chambers, at the door: "You ready?"

Chancel, crossing to the door: "Ready, willin', and able."

Chambers and Chancel come out of the Blizzard office. Chancel closes the door, and as they look in the direction of the Saunders store, they see the Slavin wagon and the Slavin boys carrying supplies out and going in for more.

Chambers: "Are they moving in, or is Saunders moving out?"

Chancel: "I don't recognize that outfit. Somebody new."

Chancel and Chambers walk toward Saunders' store. Inside, one of Slavin's boys takes the last item out, as Saunders, referring to his list says: "That does it."

Slavin nods. Saunders crosses to his counter

and starts to figure out the total as Slavin takes a pipe and tobacco from his coat pocket and starts to fill his pipe. His pouch is an old worn one made from the skin of a small animal.

Chuck is still viewing Slavin and the boys with the amused interest he has shown before. Chuck, to one of the boys: "Probably be seein' you boys at one of the dances we run every couple months or so."

The Boy, shortly, in the same laconic manner of his dad: "Reckon not."

The similarity of manner is enough to account for a little look between Saunders and Chuck. Saunders smiles to himself and goes back to his figuring.

At that moment Chancel and Chambers saunter in. By now Slavin has finished packing his pipe and lights it with an old sulphur match. As Chambers and Chancel come in, Saunders looks up and decides to go through with the amenities.

Saunders: "Slavin, this is Ned Chambers, the sheriff, and Wally Chancel, Deputy and Editor of our paper."

Chambers, amiably: "Hi."

Chancel: "How are you?"

Slavin acknowledges both greetings with just a nod as he puffs on his pipe.

Chambers, to Slavin: "Planning to stay around here?"

Slavin nods.

45

Chambers saunters over a couple of steps to the cracker barrel and dips into it. Chancel shoves his hat back on his head, takes a step or two over to a candy counter, and digs in for a free hunk.

Chancel: "You got a nice sized family."

Slavin and the boys look at Chancel.

Slavin, laconically: "Yah."

Chambers takes a step toward Slavin and looks intently at Slavin's belt buckle. Slavin becomes aware of Chambers' stare and looks down at his buckle. It is a heavy, brass confederate buckle. Embossed on it are crossed swords and the letters "C.S.A."

Chambers: "Veteran?"

Slavin looks at Chambers, Chuck, and Saunders, then nods. He takes a deep breath, motions to his boys to leave the store, then, in probably the longest speech of his life, says: "My name's Joel Slavin. Fought in the War between the States—Captain, 17th Georgia Cavalry. Left Georgia September 18, '74. Takin' over the old Nicholas place beyond the canyon. My wife's with me and my seven boys named Tom, Joe, Alec, George, John, William, and Isaac. I got my papers and my bill of sale in case the sheriff wants to see them." He looks around challengingly. "Anything else on your mind, gentlemen?"

Chancel has been practically choking on the candy he's been munching on, and Chuck hides a grin in his hand. Chambers, for a moment nonplussed by the flow of information, shakes his head no.

Slavin, to Saunders: "How much?"

Saunders: "One hundred eleven dollars and eighty-two cents."

Slavin takes out a money bag, counts out the sum in gold and silver, hands it to Saunders. Saunders makes change. Slavin takes it and puts it in his pocket.

Saunders: "Thanks for the trade."

Slavin waves an acknowledgement, goes to the front door. Reaching there, he stops, turns and looks again at the men: "I aim to stay up North —permanent." He turns and walks out, closing the door behind him.

As he leaves Saunders slaps his hands in amusement.

Chambers, ironically: "Nice friendly sort of fellow—like a grizzly."

Chuck: "Trouble with you fellows, you ain't through fightin' the Civil War."

Saunders: "I don't know, Chuck. The trouble with the Georgia Cavalryman is that you can never be sure he knows when he's beat."

Chuck: "You boys sure gave him a goin' over."

Chancel: "He did pretty well with us, too."

At just that moment Pearl comes up the steps into the store. Chambers, who has been looking out, sees her.

Chambers: "Sunrise in Homeville."

The men turn as Pearl enters. She is dressed in the beautiful plum dress that she and Chuck were talking about and is sporting something that is not very common in Homeville, a fussy bonnet adorned with artificial flowers. She turns around, preening mock-elegantly.

Chancel: "Pearl, as I look at you, I gotta admit that you're the prettiest girl—in the store at this minute."

Saunders: "I don't know if I'd go as far as to say that, Wally, but I gotta admit that she's the prettiest daughter I got."

Chuck: "Don't listen to them, Pearl. They're old-timers."

Chambers: "Pearl, that dress looks just like Boston, Massachusetts."

Pearl: "As a matter of fact it was bought in Chicago. I was maid of honor at a wedding."

Chambers: "You know, I ain't figured in a real wedding since Chuck's father got married back east almost twenty-six years ago." He looks at the others. "I don't mind sayin' I cut a pretty elegant figure. I was wearin' a velvet vest with silver buttons. I was best man."

Saunders: "If it was Matt Slattery's weddin', you wasn't the best man there."

Chancel, looking at Pearl: "You know, Pearl, you ought to stay out here with us if for no other reason—that every time we look at you we feel twenty years younger."

Saunders, with a smile: "Maybe the reason she don't want to stay is that when she looks at you she feels twenty years older."

The others smile.

Pearl: "That's very rude, Dad. The truth is I love looking at all of you."

Chuck: "Pearl, that's the nicest thing you ever said to me."

Chancel: "The place is gettin' stuffy with sentiment. Let's get goin'."

He offers his arm to Pearl. Pearl takes his arm and offers her other arm to Chuck. Chambers walks to the door and opens it with a flourish.

Saunders reaches behind the counter, takes his coat, and slips into it. He picks up the gun belt and gun from the counter and looks at them a moment. Then he walks over to the closet. As he does this the others, who are now at the front door, look back at him. Saunders hangs the gun belt and gun in the closet and closes it. He turns and looks in the direction of the others. "And there she stays." As he crosses the store toward the door where the others are waiting: "It's a nice thing to know I'll never have to put that on again."

Chancel, Pearl, and Chuck come out of the store arm in arm, followed by Chambers and Saunders. The Slavins have finished lashing all their supplies onto the wagon, and are on their horses, ready to start out.

Saunders, calling out: "Good luck, neighbor."

Slavin's pipe is clamped in his teeth. He turns and makes a little gesture of acknowledgement.

As the Slavin entourage rides down the street, the others watch them. At the back of Slavin's wagon four tools hang down from the top, suspended on leather thongs, and they shake with the motion of the wagon. These tools are a short ax, a heavy hammer, a sickle, and a short iron crowbar.

◎

Chancel, Pearl, and Chuck start down the street, followed by Chambers and Saunders. They are all in very good spirits. There is the occasional sound of a firecracker.

Saunders, to the others: "Last Fourth of July that noise wasn't coming from firecrackers." He nods. "This is a good day for all of us. In one year we got rid of the Plummer gang and Al Yunker. Yessir, it's a good day."

Chancel begins to whistle "Yankee Doodle" as they all walk down the street.

Chambers: "The only dangerous thing left around here is rattlesnakes."

There is the sound of a gun fired twice. A rattlesnake shudders as the bullets pound into him. Nearby Hygatt, Gerrett, and Gribbles sit on their horses. Gribbles holds a smoking gun in his hand. They are all looking in the direction of the snake.

Hygatt: "Fancy, Gribbles, fancy."

Hygatt spurs his horse. As he starts away the other two follow. They ride up to the crest of a hill where Hygatt pulls in his horse. The others stop alongside of him. He looks down at the section of the valley below. In the distance can be seen a large house and three or four little outbuildings.

Hygatt: "That's the place."

Gerrett: "You sure you can count on this uncle of yours?"

Hygatt: "I wouldn't have ridden seven hundred miles if I wasn't sure."

Again he spurs his horse, and the three of them start down the slope toward the Gorman ranch.

◎

Hygatt, Gerrett, and Gribbles ride up near the side of the Gorman house. The appearance of the ranch gives the impression that this could be turned into a very competent and efficient place but that it is now run down and seedy. The front yard is a mess of broken machinery, dry mud, tin cans. The entire place is littered with all sorts of junk.

As Hygatt, Gerrett, and Gribbles, walking their horses now, approach the front of the house, old man Gorman, sloppily dressed, comes out of the door. He holds a ten-gauge shotgun in his hand. A small, jolly mongrel dog named Tag comes out of the house and barks happily at the newcomers.

Gorman is an old rancher of perhaps sixty. He has a distinctly wild look in his eye.

Gorman, to the dog: "Quiet, Tag." Then to the others: "What you fellows want?"

Hygatt and the two others look down at Gorman who is standing on the front steps.

Hygatt, ingratiatingly: "H'ya, Uncle Dan."

Gorman eyes Hygatt intently.

Hygatt: "Don't you recognize me, Uncle Dan?"

Gorman: "I know who you are, and I don't want to see you." He turns away and walks back into the house, the dog following him in.

Gribbles: "He's sure glad to see you."

Hygatt: "Shut up." He gets off his horse and starts up the steps. Gerrett and Gribbles look at each other, and they slowly dismount.

The interior of the Gorman house shows the same neglect as the exterior. Gorman has come in, put the shotgun on the table, and is sitting in a chair, his hand rubbing Tag's head affectionately. He stares at the front door as Hygatt comes in.

Hygatt: "I want to talk with you, Uncle Dan."

Gorman: "Don't want to see you at all."

Hygatt walks right over to the table, sits down on it, and looks down at Uncle Dan.

Hygatt: "You look tired, and the place looks as though it needs a little repair. I'm just here to help you, that's all."

Gorman: "When I seen you eighteen years ago back in Wisconsin when you was a little shaver I told you I wanted you to come out and help me, but you didn't and now you been gallivantin' around doin' I don't know what, and here I been with no kin folk of my own since the woman died, and nobody to help me against the thieves and liars and boundary-jumpers that have been stealin' my land."

Hygatt: "If anybody's been doin' you wrong, you got to tell me about it."

Gorman, petulantly: "It's too late I told you. I'd be ownin' the whole Livin' Valley if it wasn't for them." He stands up excitedly and waves his hand indicating the outside. "Every acre belonged to me, but they scrooged and mooched and crept and stole it away from me little by little. I needed a strong right hand, a hand to smite 'em and pummel 'em, hip and thigh."

Suddenly he stops, falls back into his chair, and buries his head in his hand and sobs. The dog whines and puts his front paws up on Gorman's knees. Unseen of course by Gorman, Hygatt looks with contempt at him.

Gerrett and Gribbles saunter into the front door and stand blocking the doorway. Hygatt hears them, looks in their direction, and gives them a wise little nod. Then he reaches over and pats his uncle's shoulder.

Hygatt: "All right, Uncle Dan, all right."

Gorman straightens up, wipes his nose on his hand, and then sees Gerrett and Gribbles.

Gorman: "Who are them?"

Hygatt: "Some friends of mine. Mr. Gerrett.

Mr. Gribbles." He looks in their direction, then indicates his uncle. "This is my Uncle Dan."

Gerrett: "Hi."

Gribbles: "Hello, Uncle Dan."

Hygatt: "We're here to help. From now on, you take it easy and watch us put the place in shape."

Gorman: "There ain't much left to it, I tell you. They been tellin' me that they bought it and that they paid for it." He shakes his head and passes his hand over his eyes, obviously not clear. "I don't remember nothin' about it. I tell you that the whole Valley's mine. And now I got nothin' except this old ranch, not even a rider. I sent 'em all away because they was bleedin' me for salary." He shakes his head. "I got nothin'."

Gerrett and Gribbles exchange a look, sizing up Gorman immediately as a nut. Again he sinks to his chair.

Hygatt, putting his hand on his uncle's shoulder: "You leave everything to me."

Just then they hear a man's voice: "Mr. Gorman." Then louder: "Mr. Gorman!"

Gerrett and Gribbles and the others turn and look out. In front of the house, on the dirt road that passes it, is a buckboard pulled by two horses. In the buckboard sit Mr. and Mrs. Franson. They are a middle-aged couple. She is a strong, handsome woman, the best type of pioneer woman of this period. He is a jovial lean man. They are looking in the direction of Gorman's place.

Gorman comes out of the house, followed by Hygatt.

Franson, calling out: "You want a ride into town with us? Got room on the buckboard."

Gorman: "No, I don't want to. I'm talkin' to my nephew." He waves a dirty finger in Hygatt's direction. "This is my nephew, Arnold Hygatt. I'm talkin' to him."

Mr. Franson: "Hi."

Hygatt nods.

Franson: "See you in town."

Franson clucks to the horses, and, as the buckboard rolls away, Gorman watches the Fransons leave with murderous hate in his eyes.

Gorman: "That's the worst of them, the Franson couple. They claim they bought their place from me. I can't remember nothing. It's mine." Now he turns and grabs Hygatt's shirt front, talking to him like a crazy man. "Listen, Arnie, you stay here." Then he releases his grip and beckons to Hygatt. He crosses to the front of the porch so that he can see out all around. "All of this, the Living Valley, as far as your eye can see and more. All of it's mine—the Living Valley—room for a man to live in if you can get rid of them folks. On my northeast is Poling, a lying, cheating rat. To the southwest are them Fransons, lying hypocrites." Then he goes up close to Hygatt. "And to the southeast is Chuck Slattery."

He looks around for a moment, then very confidentially he looks at Hygatt and puts his hands on Hygatt's shirt again. "There's millions of dollars here, Arnie. My whole place is underlaid with coal, and there's lots of coal under Slattery's place which had ought to be mined, and under Franson's, and they don't know it—none of them. Nobody knows it but me, and when the railroad comes in from the east they'll pay millions for coal, Arnie, millions." Then, as if not getting enough response from Hygatt: "Millions, Arnie! Railroad's only a hundred miles from here now. All you got to do is get those cheating, dirty renegades off my land and then it's all ours, Arnie, every blessed foot of it."

Hygatt, not certain whether Gorman is crazy or not: "Sure, Uncle Dan, sure."

Gorman: "You wait here, Arnie, and we'll go and I'll show you."

He scuttles into the house. Hygatt looks at Gerrett and Gribbles who have been standing on the porch listening to everything.

Gribbles: "Maybe it ain't polite to mention it, Hygatt, but I think your uncle is crazy as a coot."

Hygatt: "Maybe."

He takes a couple of steps and looks out at the Valley that stretches north and south, his eyes almost half-closed.

Gerrett: "What're you dreaming about, Hygatt?"

Hygatt, without looking at Gerrett: "They ain't piker dreams."

Still standing there, he picks up a branding iron which is leaning against the porch railing. He hefts it in his hands, his fingers feel the branding edge. He looks at it, and then, still preoccupied, he walks down the couple of steps to the bare earth below. He pounds the branding iron into the ground half a dozen times or so. Where the branding iron has left its mark can be seen a cluster of Indian swastikas, the mark of the iron.

Gorman comes back on the porch. He has slipped on a pair of boots over his pants.

Gorman: "You can't dig gold with a branding iron. We'll get a couple of spades and a pickax, and I'll show you. I'll show you."

Hygatt joins Gorman at the bottom of the steps. Gerrett shrugs, looks at Gribbles, and they follow Hygatt and Gorman.

Gorman, Hygatt, Gerrett, and Gribbles, on horseback and followed by Tag the dog, are approaching a low rise in the foothills. Across the pommels of their saddles, Gerrett and Gribbles carry the spades and pickax. As they reach the crest of the rise, Gorman pulls his horse to a stop and points at a group of five or six dilapidated buildings. They are crude, tar-papered shanties, one storey high.

Gorman: "There it is, Moon Creek."

Gribbles: "Which one's the oprey house?"

Gorman, angrily: "Maybe there'll be one, young fellow." His hand points to the buildings below. "We started here eighteen years ago, Arnie, but the railroad was too far away, and nobody believed it would ever come, and then I needed money, and these people say that they bought my land and gave me the money, but I don't remember. But Moon Creek can be the biggest coal town west of the Alleghenies, and it belongs to me, every single inch of it, Arnie."

Hygatt: "Let's see where you was plannin' to mine."

Gorman looks at him with a smile and then chuckles: "Don't believe me even yet, do you?" He walks his horse.

The four men ride past the dilapidated buildings. The glass in the windows has long since cracked and disappeared. The doors hang from broken hinges. Several faded signs can still be seen. One of them reads, "Golden West Saloon." Another reads, "Moon Creek Mining Corporation." Another reads, "Moon Creek General Bazaar." On one side of a building in faded black letters are the words, "Office of Daniel R. Gorman, President, Moon Creek Mining Corporation."

Everywhere there is an eerie ghost-like silence broken only by the creak of the leather and the soft sound of the horses' hoofs as the four ride through the dead town.

Hygatt takes in everything he sees with deep interest. When they reach the end of the short street, Gorman pulls his horse to the left. Gorman and the others dismount, and Gorman leads them to a small hollow, sunken into the ground.

Gorman, to Gerrett: "Give me one of them spades."

Hygatt, to Gorman: "Tell him where to dig, Uncle Dan, he'll do it."

Gerrett gives Hygatt a sharp look, but with just a nod of his head Hygatt quells any incipient mutiny.

Gorman, pointing to the hollow: "Dig here."

Gerrett digs in. As he does, Hygatt turns and looks back in the direction of the city, and his eyes take in everything.

Gorman, watching Hygatt's interest: "You're

beginning to believe me, aren't you?" Again he grabs Hygatt's shirt confidentially. "With a few thousand dollars, we can get started again. The railroad will be here in less than a year."

Hygatt nods slowly, thinks this all over.

Gerrett, who now stops digging: "Now what?"

Gorman, looking at the digging: "That's enough." He steps into the hollow and reaches his hand up. "Pickax."

Gribbles hands him the pickax. Gorman swings it once or twice, then comes up with what appears to be a hard black rock. He throws it at Hygatt's feet.

Hygatt and the others crouch down to look at the rock. Hygatt wipes some of the dirt off of it. Then he looks at the other two men and nods. A smile comes over his face, and the other two show their excitement at what they see.

Hygatt gets up and turns to his uncle who is still in the hollow. He walks over and extends a helping hand to his uncle and lifts him out.

Hygatt: "Uncle Dan, you're gonna get your coal mine." He looks around. "And we'll put the paint back on them buildings, and we'll put life back in Moon Creek."

Gorman starts to sob and leans his head against Hygatt's vest. Hygatt pats him on the back.

Hygatt: "Your worries are over."

As he pats the old man's back abstractedly his face begins to glow with his private dreams of conquest.

It is now late afternoon. In the grounds in front of the Homeville school the people who live in the village and the neighbors from the surrounding ranches are all gathered around picnic tables, just finishing their picnic supper. There is a good, healthy sound of people laughing and the clatter of tinware. Five or six of the men, in their late thirties, are dressed in their Civil War uniforms for the occasion.

There is a peddler's display on the school grounds. The peddler, a grizzled Yankee, has drawn his wagon up close to the tables, and his name can be seen on its side: "Wesley Perkins—Fancy Goods—Formerly of Boston, New York, and Philadelphia."

His display on the wagon tail, which acts as a table, includes steel jewelry, brass jewelry, necklaces, patent medicine, thread and needles, darning cotton, hats and women's fancy shoes, and a few ornately jacketed books with "Gift Album" or some such title on them.

Mr. and Mrs. Franson, plus a couple of other people, are fingering some of the goods.

Perkins, the peddler, says to his prospective customers: "I won't be by here for maybe a year. You'd better load up."

Saunders watches the proceedings critically in the fashion of a great merchandiser eyeing a minor rival.

Perkins, continuing: "This is a mighty rare collection of stuff. Same kind of fancy goods purchased by Mrs. Astor in New York, sort of things you wouldn't find in these here parts."

Saunders eyes Perkins with tolerant amusement.

Mrs. Franson: "Got some pretty good values here, ain't he, Ulysses?"

Saunders, passing judgment: "Not bad for small goods at all, not bad."

Mrs. Franson has become attracted to a small hat which she now looks at speculatively. It is a distinctive looking silk hat made in the shape of a French Liberty cap. It is dark blue silk, and on one side it has an ornate red, white, and blue cockade. Mr. Franson looks at Mrs. Franson.

Franson: "What's that?"

Mrs. Franson: "It's a hat."

Franson: "Never see'd one like it."

Perkins, pressing what he believes to be a sale: "It just so happens, ma'am, you've picked the one original model in my entire stock. That was imported from Paris, France by Stewart in New York."

Mrs. Franson, very impressed: "Its very beautiful." She tries it on.

Franson looks at it now, a little more sold on the project.

Mrs. Franson, turning to Saunders: "How do you like it, 'Lysses?"

Saunders: "Nice. Becoming."

Perkins, pressing the sale: "And since there's kind of a holiday spirit in the air I'll give you a holiday price—one dollar."

Franson takes in that price, looks at Mrs. Franson. She smiles at him hopefully. Franson digs into his jeans, plunks a silver dollar on the counter.

The whitewashed walls of the interior of the school house are almost covered with pictures and mottoes, a fairly terrible old painting brought out from New England, pictures cut from *Harpers Bazaar,* biblical texts, and a couple of quotations

HYGATT

GRIBBLE

GERRETT

Mullison

Chancel

Chambers

SLAVIN

Ulysses Saunders

from Shakespeare. There are no separate school desks but five or six long benches. Shelves are built on the backs of the benches which serve as desks for the benches directly behind them. The room can seat about twenty children. In front, not on the dais, is a kitchen table for the teacher's desk with a plain kitchen chair. The entire effect is rather homelike.

Pearl and Chuck are trying to get the children in shape. The children have used the last few hours to get their costumes and faces generally messed up. They are lined up, and Pearl and Chuck are trying to make them presentable. Pearl is pinning up the costume of one little girl. Chuck is scrubbing one of the boy's faces with a roller towel. Pearl finishes her job and steps back and looks at the line of kids. She stops and shakes her head.

Pearl: "I shouldn't have let you put any of this on. Look at you."

Chuck, stepping back and eyeing them: "The whole bunch of you look as if you'd been caught in a stampede."

Pearl: "I want you all to walk out in single file to the side of the building. You're to stay there and not move, any of you."

The children all nod. "Yes, Miss Saunders," says one. "Yes, Teacher," says another.

She makes a gesture for them to walk out, and

they leave in an awkward single file. Pearl turns and looks at Chuck as the children file out.

Pearl, with a little smile: "Chuck, are you a bettin' man?"

Chuck: "On occasion."

Pearl: "I'll bet you four bits they don't get through the first chorus."

Chuck: "They're liable to surprise you." Then, a little seriously: "You know, Pearl, that's the trouble sometimes of bein' too set in your mind. You get more surprises than somebody who ain't so set."

Pearl reflects on this a moment.

Chuck, after a bit: "Are you a bettin' woman?"

Pearl, using Chuck's words deliberately: "On occasion."

Chuck: "I'll bet that if you do leave us, you'll miss all these kids. Maybe a lot of other things. Pearl, this country's gettin' civilized now, and a lot of us could use some of the education you've already got."

Pearl: "Chuck, I think this country *is* getting civilized, and I think in time it's going to grow and prosper. That's why I want to go east so that when I come back here after a while I'll be better able to help."

Chuck: "How long is 'after a while'?"

Pearl, slowly: "I don't know." Then looking in the direction of the front door and changing the subject: "We've got to get started."

She starts for the door. Chuck wants to say more but knows this is no time to continue. He follows Pearl out.

Outside the building the children are lined up. Pearl and Chuck join them.

Pearl: "All right, Chuck, you tell Mr. Chambers we're ready."

Chuck goes. Pearl changes the position of some of the children, finishes some last minute primping.

In front of the school house the children line up. Pearl goes to one side. People are seated at the benches and around the empty tables as they wait expectantly. Ulysses looks on with a little pride.

Pearl has a pitch pipe, and she blows the note. The children have been looking at her, and as they hear the note they start to sing:

"O Columbia, the Gem of the Ocean,
The home of the brave and the free . . ."

◎

Hygatt and Gorman are riding into the western edge of Homeville. The entire village, of course, seems deserted at this end. Very, very faintly in the distance they can hear the voices of the children singing:

"The shrine of each patriot's devotion,
A world offers homage to thee . . ."

Gorman, as they ride in: "I'm waiting to see all their faces when I tell them who you are and that you're going to stay with me and work the place."

Hygatt: "Don't do too much talking, Uncle Dan. I just came in to size 'em up. The talking will come later."

Gorman, chuckling: "That's smart, Arnie, smart."

As they continue up the street, the singing becomes a little clearer:

"Thy mandates make heroes assemble,
When Liberty's form stands in view.
Thy banners make tyranny tremble
When borne by the red, white and blue."

As Hygatt and Gorman ride up from the west end to the school yard, the children finish their chorus:

"When borne by the red, white and blue,
When borne by the red, white and blue,
Thy banners make tyranny tremble
When borne by the red, white and blue."

There is applause, and Pearl heaves a little sigh of relief.

Pearl: "Chuck, they did it—every word of it."

Chuck smiles, then joins in the continuing applause.

◎

At a table near the edge of the clearing are seated Mr. and Mrs. Bunny Mullison, Mullison is a big, bulky, middle-aged man. He is dressed, in rancher costume, extravagantly and in bad taste, and applauding loudly. He is a little drunk, and as he applauds, he yells: "Hooray! Hooray!"

His wide white Stetson hat is pushed back revealing a bald head. His wife, Victoria Mullison, once very pretty in a blonde way, is now a faded, thin little woman, completely dominated and abused by her husband. She lives in constant fear of him. As Bunny applauds loudly and continues calling "Hooray," Victoria looks at him a little embarrassed and then to see if others are watching.

Meanwhile Gorman and Hygatt, who have dismounted, approach the edge of the little clearing, near Mullison's table.

Mullison, seeing Gorman: "Hyah, Dan." Then expansively: "C'mon over. Take a load off your feet and set down."

He thinks this is very amusing and roars at his own good humor. His wife has a pained expression on her face at this moment and lowers her eyes in embarrassment. Gorman and Hygatt come over to the table.

Mullison: "Danny, who's the stranger with you?"

Gorman, a little stiffly: "I want you to meet my nephew, Arnold Hygatt." Then to Hygatt: "This is Mr. Bunny Mullison and his wife."

Hygatt nods. Mullison stands up and extends a big paw to Hygatt.

Mullison: "Glad to see you, son." He claps Hygatt on the back, pumping his hand at the same time. "Set down." He pushes his wife. "Move over a little, Victoria."

Victoria makes a little room. Hygatt and Mullison sit down. Mullison reaches over, grabs a tin pie plate, and slides it recklessly toward Hygatt and Gorman.

Mullison: "Put on the feed bag. Bite into a married man's pie." He laughs and nudges his wife with his elbow.

Hygatt is looking at the pie and then looks up at Mullison.

Hygatt: "Thanks. I've et."

At the table at which Saunders, Chambers, and Chancel are seated, Chambers gets up and turns to the people who are all looking at Saunders. Mullison applauds loudly and calls out: "Hooray!"

A couple of the people look over in Mullison's direction. Chancel is looking at Mullison with distaste.

Chambers: "Well, folks, I'm sure you're all proud of our little glee club, and now you're going to hear some remarks from our orator of the day, our good friend and respected citizen, Ulysses Saunders."

There is applause at this. Chambers puts his hand on Saunders' shoulder.

Mullison, calling out: "Go on, 'Lysses. Charge into them—Sixteenth Massachusetts!"

Saunders gets to his feet, faces the people, points his finger toward Mullison: "Bunny, it wasn't the Sixteenth Massachusetts, it was the Ninth. Sixteenth never saw the day it could ride along side the Ninth."

Voice from the crowd: "Who says so?"

There is a little laugh at this, Saunders lifting his hands. With a smile, he says: "I surrender. Not looking for any trouble." There is another little laugh at this.

Saunders: "Folks, I'm not much of a hand at makin' speeches. I feel a little more comfortable in back of a counter."

Mullison, yelling out: "Who's keeping their eye on the store, 'Lysses?"

Victoria pulls her husband's arm. Mullison for a moment loses his jovial expression and with the side of his hand jabs her arm away. It is a hard blow not seen by everyone, but Victoria winces and holds her arm, covering up her pain.

Saunders and some of the people who want to listen to Saunders are very annoyed with Mullison.

Saunders: "This year we got a lot to be thankful for. Law and order and peace have come to Homeville, and we're not worried any more about our homes and our belongings bein' in danger from men like Al Yunker."

Mullison gets up and pulls out his gun drunkenly.

Mullison, calling out: "Any time Al Yunker or anybody like him starts looking for trouble—" He fires two shots in the air. "Let 'em come."

There are shouts toward Mullison: "Sit down, Bunny! Shut up!"

Chancel gets up and in the little excitement talks to Chambers.

Chancel: "Bunny's gettin' playful." He walks in the direction of Bunny.

Saunders, knowing that he is not going to be able to continue his speech: "I told you I wasn't very good at speech makin', so all I want to say is I'm happy we're all here and let's hope that next year—we'll be together again—" He looks at Pearl as he says: "Every one of us."

Bunny fires another two shots in the air and yells out: "H'ray for 'Lysses Saunders."

Hygatt is looking at Mullison with studied amusement.

Mullison: "I think I'd like to make a speech too."

Victoria, whispering: "Please, Bunny, sit down."

He pays no attention to her at all.

Mullison: "Ladies and gentlemen! Last year when you were cleanin' up the Yunker gang, I happened to be down south. Now I'm a humble feller blessed with a healthy physique endowed to me by my father—rest his soul—he was a blacksmith, and I'm proud of him and I'm also endowed—" He smiles. "Also endowed with a bit of good U.S.A. currency that I got by usin' my mind." He taps his head. "A little faster than most people—" He has lost his trend of thought and hesitates a moment, then reaches down for a bottle which is on the table. He takes a swig, wipes his lips.

The people listening to Mullison are indifferent, embarrassed, and a little irritated.

Mullison puts the bottle down: "Like I said, I wasn't here to help out last time, but if the citizens of Homeville ever need my help—" He pats his gun and nods his head as if that's enough, and then continues: "While you were doing your work here, I was acting as an agent for my government in the south, makin' clear to the rebel 'secesh' that they were licked and had to knuckle under. I was a missionary of peace and victory."

Poling, a scrubby-bearded, middle-aged man, sits at another table, facing Mullison's. Not angrily, but a little defiantly, he says: "That's a fancy name for a Carpetbagger."

Mullison stops. Knowing very well, he asks: "Who said that?"

Poling: "I did!"

Mullison, swaying drunkenly: "Stand up!" His hand goes to his hip.

Chancel, followed by Chambers, comes between Poling and Mullison.

Chambers: "I think there's been enough speakin' today huh, Bunny?"

Mullison: "No man's going to insult me. Get out of the way."

Chambers: "Bunny, everybody's having a good time. Let's leave it that way."

Mullison: "If you think for a minute that I'm afraid of that star on your vest, you got another think comin', and I wouldn't care if you had twenty stars." He takes a crouching position. "Now get out!"

At that moment, just before he reaches for his gun, Hygatt, with the expert movement of a pickpocket, reaches over in back of Mullison and slides Mullison's pistol out of the holster.

Mullison reaches for his gun and looks down at his empty pocket.

Mullison, drunkenly: "Who took my gun?"

Hygatt takes Mullison by the arm and pulls him down. Mullison sits down rather heavily on the bench and looks at Hygatt. Chambers and Chancel, seeing that Mullison doesn't have his gun, turn away.

Some of the people have gotten to their feet as if anticipating trouble, and, now that it is over, there is a feeling of relaxation.

Saunders, calling out: "I got nothin' to offer the ladies, but, as far as the men are concerned, the first round at the Blackjack is on me."

There is a break of laughter here and a little chorus of thanks.

Some people walk away from the Mullison table.

Mullison, drunkenly: "Where's my gun?"

Hygatt, showing the gun to Mullison: "You see, Mr. Mullison, it seemed to me those fellows were goin' to gang up on you, and I didn't think it was fair for them to do that when you was havin' such a good time."

Mullison, thinking this over a moment, nods his head: "Uh, huh!" He's decided Hygatt did the right thing.

Mullison: "It was nice of you, young fellah." Then, confidentially: "They wouldn' dared stand in my way." He winks broadly. "If I wasn't havin' such a good time."

Hygatt, encouragingly: "I wouldn't want to be around if somebody got in your way." Then with a smile: "Unless I was on your side."

As Mullison starts to get to his feet and Hygatt helps him, we see other people moving out of the clearing in the background and Hygatt, unseen by Mullison, looks over at his Uncle Dan and gives him a wink and nods. Gorman is pleased.

Pearl, Chuck, and Saunders approach the stairway at the side of Saunders' store.

Saunders: "Goodnight, Chuck. See you soon I hope."

Chuck: "I'll be riding by in a day or two."

Saunders opens the door that leads upstairs.

Chuck, with a smile: "If you really appreciate that necktie, Mr. Saunders, you'll let me have a couple of words with Pearl."

Saunders: "Downright bribery."

Then with a little wave of farewell he walks up the steps by himself. Pearl leans against the door.

Chuck: "There just ain't enough holidays, Pearl."

Pearl: "I enjoyed today—all of it."

Chuck: "Let me ask you again, Pearl. How long is 'after a while?'"

Pearl: "I don't know yet—but I will know," she smiles, "after a while."

Chuck: "Well, it don't really make any difference how long—because I'll be waitin'."

He takes a step toward her and holds her hand.

Pearl, looking up: "Chuck, I don't know enough about what I want to do to give you any reason to wait. All I'm sure of is that I don't want to be another pioneer woman, old and bent at thirty. Maybe later on that's what I'll have to settle for, but right now I want time to think. I want to be free."

Chuck: "If you give me half a chance, Pearl, I've got more to offer you than that."

Pearl looks at him and doesn't answer. Chuck holds her hand tighter and comes closer.

Chuck, ardently: "I got this to offer, Pearl, that you haven't thought about. You want to go back east and learn something about civilization, second hand. You could stay here with me, build with me, and learn about it—first hand."

They hear the sound of horses' hoofs. Hygatt and Gorman are walking their horses up the street in the night. The moon casts their shadows toward Saunders' store.

Pearl and Chuck look off toward the street. The shadow of Hygatt's horse passes their faces. Pearl instinctively gets a little closer to Chuck. Chuck detects Pearl's fear, looks intently at Hygatt. For an instant a worried look passes over his face. Then he looks back at Pearl: "I don't like him either."

Pearl, frightened, has come very close to Chuck, whose arm is around her. Then after Chuck has spoken, he turns toward Pearl and puts his other arm around her, holding her close. Pearl, her moment of fear over, puts her hand on Chuck's chest.

Pearl, slowly but definitely: "Good-night, Chuck."

She turns quickly as Chuck releases her and goes up the steps. Chuck stands a moment looking after her, then turns and walks away.

It is daytime in Homeville. Down the street from the east comes a long, open wagon pulled by two horses. Driving the team is Gerrett. On the wagon seat beside him sits Gribbles. On a horse, alongside the wagon, rides Hygatt.

The wagon pulls up to a halt in front of Saunders' store. Hygatt dismounts from his horse, walks up the steps into the store. Gerrett and Gribbles wait in the wagon outside.

Saunders is not in the store. Hygatt looks around to see if anyone else might be there. He crosses the store and peers through the window that looks out at the back. He sees Saunders in the yard opening some boxes of merchandise with a hand ax. His sleeves are rolled up, and Hygatt gets a sense of Saunders' physical strength as he works.

Hygatt steps back from the window, obviously not wanting Saunders to see him. His eyes go to the floor above, and then he walks out.

As Hygatt comes down the steps, he gives Gerrett and Gribbles a quick gesture of silence and walks to the side of the house where the stairway is. He climbs the stairs and knocks politely on the door to the second floor. As he waits he straightens his shirt collar and adjusts his trouser belt. The door opens, and Pearl stands there.

Hygatt, flicking the brim of his hat: " 'Morning, Miss Saunders."

Pearl: " 'Morning."

Hygatt takes a step toward the door. Pearl makes no effort to invite him in and stands more or less blocking him.

Hygatt: "I didn't mean to disturb you. I was just lookin' for your father."

Pearl: "You'll find him in the back, Mr. Hygatt."

Hygatt, with a nod: "Thank you." He looks in at the living room. "You got your place fixed up pretty. Haven't seen a parlor organ like that since I was a young fellow." Then, as he steps into the room: "Mind if I look around?"

Pearl remains at the door as Hygatt steps in and removes his hat. His manner is an attempt to be very ingratiating.

Hygatt: "There's no doubt about it. You can always tell a lady's hand in a room like this." He looks at Pearl. "Mind if I pay you a compliment, Miss Saunders?" Then, without waiting for an answer: "I been in a lot of places all through the east and Mexico and Cuba and California." He smiles. "Some mighty fashionable homes, too —but you'd give them kings and aces."

Pearl: "Thank you, Mr. Hygatt." Then, not curtly, but changing the subject: "You'll find my father in the back yard."

Hygatt turns, looks at her, and is shrewd enough to know that Pearl doesn't like him. He strolls toward the door.

Hygatt, as he does this: "Thanks for your courtesies, Miss Saunders."

As Hygatt reaches the door he stops and looks at Pearl who has hardly moved from the door where she originally stood.

Hygatt: "I've only been here about three weeks, Miss Saunders, and it takes more than that to get acquainted around these parts." He looks at her. "I have a feeling that you're either suspicious of me or afraid of me." He smiles. "I make it a policy never to trust my first impressions." Pearl just nods. He flicks his hat brim again. Then, with a smile: "Thanks for the nice talk, Miss Saunders."

He walks out and down the steps. He no longer smiles. He is miffed, hurt, and annoyed. Above him Pearl looks down at his retreating figure for a moment and then slams the door as she goes back into the living room.

Inside the store Hygatt is standing in front of the counter while Saunders figures up the sum that Hygatt owes him. Outside Gerrett and Gribbles finish the loading of supplies they have bought.

Saunders, looking up: "Now, was there anything else?"

Hygatt, shaking his head: "No, I think I can get plenty done with what I got on the wagon now."

Saunders, pleasantly: "You're going to be a big help to your uncle. He was letting his place get mighty seedy."

Hygatt: "Well, Uncle Dan's kind of an old man. He wastes a little too much time talking about all the mean things that his neighbors have done to him." He smiles. "I don't pay him much mind."

Saunders: "That's usin' good sense. We never had much of a chance to do any talkin', Hygatt, and maybe you don't know that your uncle's been kind of a troublemaker around here. Al Yunker, one of the worse road agents we ever had around these parts, used to work for your uncle as a foreman. When we finally got after Yunker, we had to shoot up your uncle's place a little to get him out of there. And if you want to question any of the deals that your uncle made you'll find them all on record. Nobody cheated him." He points a finger at the safe in back of him. "They're all listed there in the county deed book."

Hygatt: "I know. I'm just aimin' to put his ranch on a payin' basis and tryin' to get things done."

Saunders, with a little nod: "And I think you will."

Just then Pearl comes into the store. Hygatt again flicks the brim of his hat.

Saunders: "You met my daughter, haven't you?"

Hygatt: "Sure, Mr. Saunders. We had a little talk just before you came into the store." Then, looking at Saunders' statement: "What's it all come to?"

Saunders: "One hundred eighty dollars and eighty cents."

Hygatt: "I've only got fifty dollars cash. I'll give you a note for the rest."

Saunders: "I never refuse anybody credit—the first time." He turns to Pearl. "Will you make out a note, Pearl—one hundred thirty dollars and eighty cents at the regular rate of interest."

Hygatt nods. Pearl steps in back of the counter, and, taking a pen and ink, fills out a note. During this, Saunders looks at Hygatt.

Saunders: "You puttin' in any new stock?"

Hygatt: "Aim to. Got a lot of ideas. This newcomer north of us, Slavin, has got a mighty big place, and I don't want him swampin' the rest of us."

Saunders: "Nothing like good healthy competition."

By this time, Pearl has finished making out the note. She hands the pen to Hygatt who takes it and scratches a signature. Saunders takes a look at it just to be sure Pearl made it out all right. Hygatt nods a pleasant farewell and starts out of the door.

Hygatt, just before he leaves: "Appreciate your kindness, Mr. Saunders."

As Hygatt walks out of the store, Saunders looks at Pearl.

Saunders, mock-seriously: "You know, Pearl, I didn't hear a word you said. You might have been a little bit more neighborly to a good customer."

Pearl: "I don't like him, Dad."

Saunders: "If I was to try and run a business by the look of a man's face I wouldn't be doin' very well. You know there ain't very many handsome people around here, Pearl."

Pearl: "There's something evil about him."

Saunders: "Nothin' evil about him if he pays that note on time. There's only one way to judge a man's character—by his credit."

Pearl: "I won't argue with you, Dad. You built this business up from a powder horn and a package of needles—maybe you're right."

Saunders, putting his arms around her: "Ain't I always?"

Pearl, smiling up at him: "But if I'm right, you'll find out that you can't do business with Hygatt."

Outside the Saunders' store, Gerrett and Gribbles have finished packing in the supplies. They are seated again on the wagon seat. As Hygatt comes out, a scraggly-bearded, dirty loafer named Quist saunters up and looks at the crowded wagon and at Hygatt. He approaches Hygatt.

Quist, through his dried brown spittle: "You need a hand to help you with the load, Boss?"

Hygatt: "It's all loaded."

Quist, with a broken-toothed grin: "That's why I wanted to help."

Hygatt continues toward his horse. Quist hangs on right at his heels.

Quist: "I've been huntin' gold west of here, and for twenty dollars grubstake I'll make you my partner."

Hygatt brushes him off: "Gold is the root of all evil."

Quist, with the same grin: "Maybe so, but twenty dollars of evil would do me a lot of good."

Hygatt digs into his pocket and gives Quist a silver coin: "Go buy yourself a pipe dream."

Quist: "Thank you, thank you. My name's Quist, if you ever need a friend."

Hygatt stops, looks at him: "My name's Hygatt. You remember it—and if you ever hear anybody use it in a way you think I mightn't like, let me know."

Quist: "Thank you, Boss, I will."

Hygatt mounts his horse and waves a little salute to Quist. This salute is a flat-handed salute. Quist looks up at him and waves the same kind of answering salute. Hygatt, followed by the wagon driven by Gerrett and Gribbles, rides away from Saunders' store.

Gorman's ranch has been cleaned up to a good extent. The wagon has been unloaded. The new supplies are in an orderly heap.

Old man Gorman has unharnessed the horses. Gerrett and Gribbles are sorting out the supplies. Hygatt is working on the top of the porch in front of the house with a can of paint and a brush. He is standing on a short ladder which leans against the house. Gorman, leading the horses, crosses over near Hygatt.

Gorman, looking up at Hygatt: "Arnie, who's going to pay for all this here stuff you're buyin', and what good's it going to do?"

Hygatt: "There's a lot of work to be done, and too many questions just waste time."

Gorman, petulantly: "Now just a minute, Arnie. I ain't just a hired hand around this place."

Gerrett, to Gorman: "Aw, shut up and get the horses into the barn."

Gorman looks at him furiously.

Hygatt, impatiently: "Go on, go on."

Gorman leads the horses away.

Gribbles, to Hygatt, as he starts to lift a box: "All of this has got the smell of too much honest work—I don't like it." Sardonically: "I do despise work."

Hygatt: "D'you ever write a will, Gribbles?"

Gribbles, putting down the box: "No, but it sounds more interestin' than carryin' boxes."

Hygatt, as he paints: "When you get a little spare time, you ought to draw up my uncle's last will and testament, leaving everything to his lovin' nephew Arnold Hygatt." Then mock-sympathetically: "Uncle's gettin' mighty old, and he might neglect it before he dies."

Gerrett: "That's very thoughtful of you, Boss —but maybe your uncle won't want to sign it."

Hygatt: "He will."

Gerrett, slyly: "He might not die."

Hygatt: "He will."

Gorman, followed by his dog Tag, comes from around the side of the house. Gribbles has turned to lift a package, and Tag runs up near Gribbles and snaps playfully at his boot. Gribbles gives him a little kick to one side. Tag, thinking that he's playing, comes back at him.

Gribbles, to Gerrett: "Get rid of that pup, will you?"

Gerrett smiles, leans over to a bucket of paint which is perched on the porch railing with a brush inside. He lifts the brush and throws it at Tag. As Tag is hit by the paint brush it splatters dark green paint all over him into his eyes and face. Tag yaps.

As Gorman bends down to the whimpering dog he looks up at Gerrett.

Gorman: "That's a cowardly thing for a man to do."

He lifts the whimpering dog in his arms. Still holding Tag, he comes to the side of the house where a bucket of water, a brush, and soap stand. As he begins to wash the dog he mumbles softly: "They hadn't oughta do that to you. We never should have let them come here, Tag. All they been doin' is spendin' my money and yellin' at the both of us—oughta drive 'em away from here, that's what we oughta do."

Tag has tried to get a little loose from Gorman as Gorman has been washing him, and Gorman gives him a sharp, hard knock over the nose.

Gorman: "Stand still." He continues washing the dog.

Down the road toward the house comes a magnificent white horse, and on the horse is Bunny Mullison, elaborately dressed. His boots are ornate, his saddle expensive. He wears a black shirt and a big black Stetson with a silver band around it. As he approaches the house he calls out: "Hi."

Mullison rides his horse close up to the porch and remains seated. Gerrett and Gribbles wave a salute, and Hygatt gets off the ladder and wipes his hands on some waste.

Hygatt: "Hello, Mr. Mullison."

Mullison: "I don't feel I've been very neighborly. You've been here over three weeks, and I never come by to say thank you for bein' so friendly at the picnic."

Hygatt: "Glad you dropped by."

Mullison, his eyes going over the part of the ranch he can see: "You're goin' to have a first class ranch before you know it."

Hygatt: "Not much interested ranchin'. I got other plans."

This piques Mullison's interest: "Around these parts, what other plans could you have but ranchin'?"

Just then Gorman comes in from the side of the house again with Tag in his arms. He's finished cleaning the pup up.

Mullison, with a little salute: "Hello, Mr. Gorman."

Gorman, ignoring Mullison's hello and talking to Gerrett and Gribbles: "Now, listen, you fellows, if any one of you ever puts a hand on my dog again—"

Hygatt, sharply, to Gorman: "Get into the house." He puts his hand on Gorman's shoulder and gives him a push toward the porch. "Get in and keep your fool mouth shut."

Mullison takes this in with great interest. Gorman goes into the house.

Mullison, casually: "You're mighty fond of your uncle."

Hygatt: "A lot of men, when they get over seventy, don't know much about what's good for them."

Mullison, leaning forward: "I was askin' what other plans you got."

Hygatt looks up at Mullison a moment. This is an important step he's about to take and, in some respects, a risky one.

Hygatt, slowly: "How near has the buildin' of the railroad got to Homeville?"

Mullison, sure of his answer: "About a hundred mile."

Hygatt: "They're goin' to need lots of coal when they come through here."

Mullison nods.

Hygatt: "If a fellow had the coal to sell 'em—" He stops.

Mullison, eyeing him for a moment, slowly gets off his horse.

Hygatt: "You sure I ain't keepin' you, Mr.

Mullison, from something more important?"

Mullison, as he throws his reins to the ground: "You know you ain't."

Hygatt walks away from the front of the house to the far side that overlooks the old forgotten city of Moon Creek. Mullison follows him over. Gerrett and Gribbles exchange a look, but stay behind.

Hygatt, pointing off in the direction of Moon Creek: "There's a vein of coal runs through there, Mr. Mullison. Nobody knows how deep, nobody knows how much—but it can mean millions."

Mullison, not tipping his mitt too quickly: "If what you say is so, that vein's liable to spread into Slattery's place and Franson's and Poling's."

Hygatt: "Maybe. But they don't know it, or don't believe it. Nobody knows but me—and now, you. With a little cooperation and a little money—"

Mullison, his eyes beginning to light up with a little enthusiasm: "Sounds kind of dazzling, Mr. Hygatt."

Hygatt nods his head: "And if you got imagination, Mr. Mullison, you can even dream about the day when maybe two enterprisin' fellows could own Mr. Slattery's place and Poling's and Franson's and all of the Living Valley."

Mullison: "I got imagination." He extends his hand to Hygatt. Hygatt shakes it.

Hygatt, with a little smile: "And you got money."

Mullison thinks this is a very funny joke. He starts to laugh and pumps Hygatt's hand.

Chuck Slattery is sawing a plank. Pearl steadies the other edge. Chuck finishes sawing through the plank, and Pearl almost loses her balance as the wood parts. Chuck drops the saw and steadies her. He smiles.

Chuck: "You had a mighty good grip on that."

Pearl smiles. Chuck puts down the plank he has just sawed and places another one on the wooden horses: "I'm glad that Pete's building that church—not that I'm a very religious fellow, but I like the idea of you coming out here to help him."

Pearl: "I want to see the church finished before I go east." She looks at Chuck. "Just to prove to you that I can build something—firsthand."

Just then Peterson comes from around the side of the ranch house: "If you got some of those planks sawed we ought to try and get 'em up."

Chuck: "Well, we got a couple of them ready."

Peterson: "We better get 'em up. Want to be

sure to get that roof finished before the rains come." He looks down at Chuck and Pearl for a minute. "I get torn between two thorns—if I pray for the rain to come so the grass will be green, it'll ruin the church—and if I pray for the rain to stay away till I get the church finished, it's no good for the grass."

Pearl: "Well, how do you get out of that situation, Reverend?"

Peterson, with a little shrug: "I've decided to leave it all to nature, but to get the roof on quick."

They laugh and start for the church that Peterson has been building on Chuck's ranch. It is a crude, clapboard affair. Its seating capacity when finished will be about forty. One side of the roof has already been finished.

Peterson braces himself on the other side of the roof, fitting into place a plank which Chuck hands up to him. Chuck is perched on a ladder and receives the plank from Pearl who is standing on the ground. As Peterson puts the plank in place, he hammers a couple of nails to hold it, then they slide over to receive the next plank which Pearl lifts and hands up. Pearl has a little difficulty with this one because she is a little off-balance. She staggers.

Chuck, warningly: "You all right? Take it easy! Look out!"

Pearl catches her balance and lets the plank fall into Chuck's hands. As Chuck slips it up to Peterson and Peterson hammers it in place, Chuck's eyes are taken by something in the disstance. He points his finger.

Chuck, to Pearl: "We got company." Pearl looks up.

An open wagon pulled by two horses has rolled up in front of Chuck's house. Sheriff Chambers is driving the team of horses. Alongside of him sits Mrs. Chambers. Wally Chancel on horseback has ridden along with them. As Chancel waves to Chuck and as Chambers guides the wagon toward the church, Pearl walks toward the wagon and Chuck helps Peterson down from the roof. They then walk over to the front of the church where the wagon has stopped. Chancel dismounts.

Chambers: "Hi, folks!"

Mrs. Chambers: "Hello, everyone."

Chambers, to Peterson: "Mrs. Chambers took it upon herself to gather a few donations, and with the money we had some benches built for the church."

Peterson: "Thank you all kindly, and bless you."

Mrs. Chambers: "It's the least we can do, Reverend. It's about time we had a church around here."

Chancel: "Bein' by nature a practical man I'd

like to suggest we get the benches into the church."

The others smile and nod as everyone busies himself taking the benches into the church.

◎

Inside the church the light streams in directly from above through the half-finished roof. Mrs. Chambers and Pearl are putting the benches in an orderly line, and Chancel and Chuck are carrying in a bench, followed by Peterson and Chambers who are bringing in another one. They put them down.

Chuck: "That's all of it, Pete."

Peterson looks with pride at the benches. He is standing in the place where he hopes the altar will be eventually. The light streams down on his white head. He looks up a moment, and his hands go out in a gesture of benediction. The others bow their heads, the men removing their hats. Peterson voices an inaudible prayer, and at the conclusion he lowers his hands.

Suddenly the people in the church hear the clatter of horses' hoofs. As everyone becomes aware of the noise and looks out of the church, Gerrett slides his horse to a quick stop and calls out: "Sheriff Chambers here?"

People come out of the church.

Chambers: "Yeah?"

Gerrett remains seated on his horse. Chancel moves close to Chambers.

Gerrett: "There's been an accident."

Chancel: "What kind of an accident?"

Gerrett: "Mr. Gorman had a fall—there bein' no doctor nor nothin' Mr. Hygatt figured we ought to get hold of you. It's serious."

Chambers, to Chuck: "Can I borrow a horse, Chuck?"

Chuck nods.

Peterson: "I'll get it." He goes to saddle the horse.

Pearl: "I'll drive home with Mrs. Chambers."

Chancel has continued looking at Gerrett. Gerrett becomes aware of Chancel's stare and looks down at him.

Gerrett: "My name is Gerrett."

Chancel, eyeing him blankly: "Hi."

Gerrett, just as flatly: "Hi."

There is an unspoken challenge between both these men as they look at each other, sizing each other up.

At the Gorman ranch Gribbles sits on the railing of the front porch. The dog Tag sits near Gorman's body. Hygatt stands looking down at the body of Gorman which is stretched on the ground. Hygatt looks up as the sound of horses is heard and Chambers, Chancel, and Gerrett ride up. The men dismount quickly. Chambers, as sheriff, takes over. They cross to the body of Gorman. Chambers bends toward the body and puts his hand on Gorman's heart. He looks up.

Chambers: "How long ago did he die?"

Hygatt: "Couple of hours ago, I guess."

As Chambers stands up, Chancel bends down to examine the body of Gorman. As he does, Gerrett runs his fingers over his lip, and watching Chancel, flexes his fingers as if choking someone and then allows them to relax.

Hygatt, rubbing his hand over his eyes as if weathering a shock: "It's almost unbelievable, Sheriff." He shakes his head.

Chambers: "How'd it happen?"

Hygatt: "Well, we finished up the day's chores and sat down to have a couple of drinks, when Uncle began to talk—like he always did—about the way people had been cheatin' him, and before any of us could stop him, he ran out sayin' he was gonna have a showdown. Next thing we heard was a yell, and we come out here and he was layin' there just like you see him. He must have tripped on one of the steps. I sent Gerrett out for some help because I seen he was hurt serious, and then after a little while—he died."

Chambers: "Without knowin' too much about it, I'd say his neck was broke."

Gribbles, still seated on the rail: "That's what it looked like to me."

Chancel: "What'd you leave him layin' out here in the dirt for?"

Hygatt: "We tried to move him in, but every time we touched him he asked us not to move him. It hurt too much."

Chancel: "You could have given him a decent place to lie when he was dead."

Tag whines occasionally.

Hygatt: "We were just goin' to do that when you rode up."

Chambers, shaking his head, looks at Hygatt: "Your Uncle Dan was a fine old pioneer gentleman—you have my sympathies, Mr. Hygatt."

Hygatt nods, too full of grief to answer.

Chambers, with a deep sigh: "Well, there's nothin' much more to say. You can make your own funeral arrangements, and I'll fill out the report."

Hygatt, to Gerrett: "Let's take him in the house."

As Hygatt and Gerrett bend down to lift Uncle Dan's body, Tag whines and follows them into the house.

◎

Chambers and Chancel ride down the road away from Gorman's place. They walk their horses. Chancel is talking to Chambers. Chambers apparently doesn't agree with Chancel.

Chambers: "Wally, you know that Gorman was always gettin' himself excited. It is just the sort of thing that could have happened to him. The old man might have slipped just like they say."

Chancel: "Just don't seem natural to me that they would let him lay out there."

Chambers: "Well, they didn't know what to do."

Chancel: "That's my point. I think they did know what to do. They wanted the law to see just how it happened so that there wouldn't be any questions asked."

Chambers suddenly pulls his horse to a stop and looks at Chancel with sharp surprise.

Chambers: "Are you sayin' that they killed him?"

Chancel: "I'm sayin' it's possible that they did—I don't like that Hygatt, and I don't like his two friends."

Chambers, shaking his head: "Wally, you're takin' this deputy job too serious."

Chancel: "Ned, you got to stop thinkin' that just because you're in favor of law and order and peace that everybody feels the same way you do."

Chambers waves a disinterested hand at Chancel and spurs his horse.

On a stretch of range land, Hygatt, riding by himself, approaches a group far in the distance. Mullison and three of his riders are gathered around a small fire, branding some calves. Mullison looks up as Hygatt approaches. Hygatt waves a salute and dismounts.

Hygatt: "Howdy, Mr. Mullison."

Mullison: "Glad to see you."

Hygatt: "You got a little time?"

Mullison, with a nod: "Yeah." He turns to his men. "Keep at it, boys." He takes Hygatt's arm, and they walk a little distance away.

Mullison, with a nod of his head indicating the men behind them: "You got to keep after men workin' for you. That's the only way you get things done on time, and one thing about my place, Hygatt, everything always runs on time."

Hygatt: "I figured you for a thorough man, Mr. Mullison."

Mullison: "Heard about your poor uncle."

Hygatt: "Yeah—happened right after he signed the will leavin' everything to me."

Mullison, with a knowing look: "Tsk, tsk."

Hygatt: "There are a lot of things got to be done and done fast—I need three thousand dollars to begin with."

Mullison, a little taken aback: "Holy cat!"

Hygatt: "After we get supplies and start work at the mine the first thing I got to do is prove that my dear old dead uncle had a prior claim on Chuck Slattery's land—and now that my uncle's dead it really belongs to me."

Mullison: "When are you gonna prove that?"

Hygatt: "In a couple of days, as soon as Gerrett and Gribbles have made the necessary arrangements."

Mullison: "If you intend takin' over Chuck Slattery's ranch, your first 'necessary arrangements' better be a gun."

Hygatt, with a smile: "The pen is mightier than the sword." Then, chewing on a blade of grass that he has picked up: "People around here are mighty law abidin', and if the law is on our side we won't need any guns—not yet."

Mullison: "When do you need the money?"

Hygatt: "Now."

Mullison: "Speakin' of bein' law abidin', I

want you to sign a little paper showin' that we're partners. Fifty-fifty."

Hygatt nods.

Mullison: "And this paper'll be the real thing—sorta the axis that the whole thing turns around." He makes a descriptive gesture, and he slaps Hygatt on the back. "Now come up to my place and we'll have a drink on it."

◎

It is night. Near a clump of trees outside Homeville, Hygatt, protected by the shadows of the trees, sits on his horse. Gerrett and Gribbles accompany him.

Hygatt, snapping his fingers: "Get goin'!"

Still seated on their horses, Gerrett and Gribbles remove their spurs. Then they dismount and steal toward town on foot, Hygatt holding their horses.

The silent shadowy figure of Gerrett and Gribbles approach Saunders' store. Without a sound they open the back door, enter, and close the door behind them. They move over in the direction of the safe.

They look at the safe, Gribbles' fingers feeling the round dial. He looks up at Gerrett with a smile.

Gribbles, whispering: "A cheesebox." His fingers go to work on the dial.

Gribbles opens the safe, takes out a large folio, and beckons to Gerrett. They steal from behind the counter to the other side of the store, hiding themselves behind some large cases of supplies.

Gribbles seats himself tailor-fashion on the floor. He digs into his pockets, takes out a candle, and puts it on the floor beside him. Gerrett shields the top of the candle with his hat as Gribbles strikes a match and lights the candle. He then opens the folio and looks through some of the pages.

Gribbles, very quietly: "Child's play."

He reaches into a chest pocket, pulls out a couple of vials of ink, and examines them in the candlelight, and then he reaches for a pen also tucked away in his pocket.

Gerrett and Gribbles finish their work, put everything in order, then close the door at the rear of the place, softly. They relock the door and steal down the steps.

They return quietly to the clump of trees where Hygatt waits. As they get on their horses and begin to rearrange their spurs, Hygatt looks at them intently: "Well?"

Gribbles, with a hard smile: "As the sole heir of Daniel Gorman you are now by prior purchase the owner of Chuck Slattery's ranch."

Gerrett, with a hard smile to Hygatt: "Congratulations."

Hygatt just beckons with his head. The three men spur their horses and ride swiftly off.

At the Slattery ranch, Chuck apparently has visitors. Three horses are standing outside his house. Inside, the house is a simply furnished place. Chuck is standing, his back to a small iron coal heating stove. Facing him are three visitors, Saunders, Chambers, and Chancel. Saunders is half-seated on a table. Chambers is standing facing Chuck, and Chancel is seated in one of the chairs.

Chuck, heatedly: "There's no sense of my goin' to town 'cause if I seen it written in ten books I wouldn't believe it."

Chambers: "Chuck, you believe we're your friends, don't you?"

Chuck: "Right now I believe only one thing—this is my ranch, and it was my father's, and I'm goin' to stay here no matter what you seen written in a record book."

Saunders: "Like I said, it was only this

mornin' that Hygatt came in. He paid off a note he owed me—every cent of it and then got to talkin' about his uncle—you know as well as we do, Chuck, that his uncle was always claimin' something or other. Hygatt was just statin' his rights when he said he wanted to see the record, so I called Ned here and Wally, and we opened the safe and there it was, in black and white—old man League's handwritin'—written jes' like he used to write everything before he died."

Chuck: "I don't care if it's written in black or white or red or green and whether it was written by League or his ghost. I say it ain't true and it was written there recent."

Chambers: "We looked at it through a magnifyin' glass, and it all stands up, Chuck."

Chancel: "It's like they say, boy—I feel like you do, but I don't know what you can do about it."

Chuck: "I know what I can do. I'm stayin' here, and the first man that tries to move me whether it's one of you fellas or Hygatt or anybody is gonna get shot dead for trespassin'."

Chambers: "Chuck, when your father died I promised I'd watch out for you. Hygatt's got the law on his side, and your standin' up like this against him means you're committin' suicide. According to the law, from this minute on you're the one that's trespassin' on his land."

Chuck turns quickly to the gun belt that's hanging on the wall near him and whips out his forty-four: "Get outa here—go on!"

Saunders sits back on the table and scratches his head: "Chuck, I don't blame you for bein' riled. We'll try and figure somethin' out to help you."

Chuck, steadily: "Get out of here!"

Chancel gets up and walks out. Chambers looks at Chuck a moment, makes a half attempt to say something, changes his mind and walks out.

Saunders, as he straightens himself up again, looks at Chuck: "I think you ought to talk this over with Pearl."

Chuck: "Nothin's changin' my mind."

Saunders, putting his hands in his back pockets: "You oughta talk to her, son—she's on your side." He slowly walks out.

Near a thin little creek Saunders and Chambers are standing as their horses rest and drink. Chancel sits on the sparse grass, puffing on a cigar.

Chambers: "I think we oughta have a talk with Hygatt. Maybe he'd listen to reason. Maybe we can buy Chuck's place without him knowin' anything about it and tell him that Hygatt changed his mind."

Chancel: "Hygatt wants Chuck's place too bad to sell."

Saunders: "Everything's got its price." He looks at Chambers. "You have a talk with Hygatt and see what he'd take—you can count me in for whatever it costs."

Chambers: "Instead of me sendin' for Hygatt, I think I'll ride over to Moon Creek and have a talk with him."

Chancel: "If you're ridin' to Moon Creek you can ride alone. I'm not goin' with you."

Chambers: "I'll drop by Franson's place and pick him up—he feels like we do."

Saunders: "I'll stay out of this as far as Hygatt goes. You do the talking."

Chambers, walking over to his horse: "You know if we challenge Hygatt and try to carry this to the courts he's liable to shoot first and ask questions later."

Chancel: "If there's to be shootin', let it come now." He gets up and points a cigar at Chambers. "You mark my words, Ned. The longer you put off the shootin' the more shootin' there's goin' to be." Then looking at Saunders with the same aggressive assurance: "And no matter whether he pays you his bills or not, 'Lysses,—you can remember what I tell you. You can't do business with Hygatt."

Chambers, who has stopped and looked at Chancel, now turns and slowly mounts his horse. He looks down at Chancel and Saunders: "There's been enough shootin' and enough killin'—I'm ridin' to Moon Creek."

He pulls his horse's head to one side, and as he rides off, Chancel and Saunders mount their horses and ride the other way.

Some of the ghostly aspects of Moon Creek have already disappeared. Gerrett and Gribbles working some of Mullison's men have begun the cleaning up process. New lumber is stacked in the streets, fresh paint is going up on a couple of the buildings, and a few horses and a couple of wagons are visible.

Chambers and Franson are riding into town. Their eyes are taking in with interest all that they see. Franson nudges Chambers and points. Chambers looks. There is an excavation near where Gorman dug out the coal. This excavation is the beginning of a large open pit.

Franson: "I think our friend is going in for wagon mining."

Chambers, questioningly: "What kind of mine?"

Franson: "Old man Gorman always said there was coal around here."

Chambers nods sadly. He and Franson pull up their horses near one of the buildings. Two of Mullison's men are hammering a section of wood walk in front of the building.

Chambers: "Where can I find Mr. Hygatt?"

One of the Men: "He's in the back—in the office."

Chambers and Franson dismount. They look with interest at a large sign over the door which reads:

THE TWO AXES MINING COMPANY

Behind the lettering is painted a crude picture of two crossed axes. After Chambers and Franson read the sign, they continue on in.

No one is at work inside right now, but what is taking shape is a large office for the mining company, a long counter on one side, a couple of rude desks, homemade, a paymaster window, and in the back, an office.

Chambers and Franson, beginning to be astonished, continue down toward the office. Chambers opens the door. In the office sit Mullison and Hygatt. This office is fitted up unusually well and is a final surprise to Chambers and Franson. On the wall is a surveyor's map. Mullison and Hygatt, who rise as Chambers and Franson come in, have the smug assurance that comes with the realization that they have an "ace in the hole."

Hygatt waves a little salute.

Mullison: "Hi, Sheriff, Franson!"

Franson nods.

Chambers, to Hygatt: "This is Mr. Franson."

Hygatt: "We met."

Franson: "Yeah, I remember."

Chambers: "I want to have a little talk with you, Hygatt—sort of private."

Hygatt: "This is private." He indicates Mullison. "Mr. Mullison and me are partners now. Anything you got to say to me goes for him."

Chambers is a little surprised.

Franson: "What d'you plan to be partners in?"

Hygatt: "The coal minin' business. A new city is gonna rise here—a real city."

Mullison: "It's gonna be good not only for us but for everybody around here—bring prosperity into the neighborhood."

Chambers, a little skeptically: "Well, **good** luck to both of you."

Hygatt, leaning forward: "You don't believe that, do you?" He points a finger. "Well, let me tell you something, Chambers. You're gonna see things that you never saw before. Now that Mullison and me are in a position to develop this valley we're gonna make kind of a new world—there's gonna be a new order of things around here."

Franson: "You're an ambitious man, Mr. Hygatt."

Hygatt: "Anything wrong with that?"

Franson shrugs.

Hygatt: "Take a look around. See for yourself."

Chambers: "Hygatt, what I wanted to talk to you about is Chuck Slattery."

Hygatt, shortly: "We covered that this mornin'."

Chambers: "I wanted to discuss with you the possibility of buyin' Chuck's property from you at a price that you might consider fair."

Hygatt, nodding his head as if considering the proposition: "Well, that makes kind of good sense." He turns to Mullison. "Remember, Bunny, we sort of considered this this morning." He turns to Chambers. "Price is a million dollars."

Franson: "We didn't ride out for jokes."

Hygatt: "Maybe you got a better sense of humor than me, Mr. Franson. I wasn't jokin'." He turns to Chambers. "Slattery by rights has been trespassin' on my property for over twenty years, gettin' it stunk up with cattle—now it's mine legal, and you know it as well as I do. There's nothin' to talk about, and I don't want to listen to any sentimental hogwash about young Mr. Chuck."

Franson, knowing further talk is useless: "We got a long ride back, Sheriff, and it's gettin' late."

Hygatt: "Before you go I want to remind you about my rights, and if Chuck or any of his friends decided to challenge my rights—they ain't got much of a future."

Chambers: "There won't be any shootin'—the law's the law, and it's my job to enforce it —whether I like it or not."

He and Franson start for the door.

Mullison: "You see, Sheriff, we're not lookin' for trouble—we're just stickin' to our rights."

Chambers turns.

Hygatt: "It isn't like I was askin' for something that wasn't mine—Chuck Slattery's ranch is all I want."

Chambers nods.

Hygatt, quickly: "Wednesday morning, eight o'clock sharp, I move in."

Chambers nods, and he and Franson go to the door and exit.

Mullison, slapping his thigh: "Did you get a look at their faces—" He slaps Hygatt on the back "Signed, sealed, and delivered."

Hygatt crosses to the map.

Hygatt: "The valley's ours, Bunny." His finger indicates Living Valley on the map which bears a strong resemblance to the map of the European continent.

Hygatt: "But it's just the beginning; Mr. Franson don't know it, but he's just sat in at his own funeral." He points his finger to the Franson place. "And with him was Poling and Norton and Belger and Slavin—all of 'em."

As he stops they hear the whining of a dog. They look toward the window of the office. Hygatt, taking out his gun, crosses to the window. Outside the window, wee Tag, sitting on his haunches, is whining unhappily. Hygatt reaches to the desk and throws a lump of coal at Tag. The dog starts to move away. As he does, Hygatt takes out his revolver and levels it. There is the sound of two shots. The dog collapses in a heap.

Hygatt turns away from the window, putting his revolver back in his holster.

Hygatt, to Mullison: "I like to give 'em an even chance of runnin' away."

Mullison, not quite as happy as Hygatt, nods.

Chambers and Pearl are riding toward the Slattery ranch. The sun is just coming up. In front of Chuck's place, Slavin and his three eldest sons stand relaxed with their rifles under their arms. They look up with interest, their faces set for trouble as Chambers and Pearl ride up to the ranch.

Slavin, calling into the house: "Slattery!"

Chuck comes out wearing a heavy belt of cartridges and his revolver. He holds a repeating rifle in his hands.

Chambers and Pearl dismount and walk toward Chuck.

They pass Slavin and his three sons. Slavin politely flicks the brim of his hat.

Chambers, to Slavin as they go by: "Hello, Slavin."

Slavin nods. Pearl and Chambers come up to Chuck. Slavin stands motionless.

Chuck, to Chambers: "It's Wednesday morning, Sheriff, and in two and a half hours Hygatt'll be here. All the talkin's been done."

Pearl: "I haven't done any of the talking, Chuck—that's why I'm here."

Chuck: "You'd better go back, too."

Chambers: "Look, boy, can't you see what you're doin'?" He indicates Slavin with his finger. "If the shooting starts, people are goin' to take up sides. Men are goin' to die. Land isn't worth that."

Chuck: "I didn't ask Slavin or anybody else here."

Chambers: "If I wanted to I could have had twenty men ride with me to help you fight off Hygatt, and before you know it we would have a nice private little war going on." He shakes his head. "There's been enough of that."

Chuck: "Go on home, Sheriff, and let me be." He looks at Pearl. "And you too." He turns and walks into the house.

Pearl and Chambers look at each other, and Pearl whispers to Chambers: "You go on back—wait for me at the creek." Then, self-assuredly: "I'll be there."

She walks into the house after Chuck. Chambers hesitates a minute, then walks down the steps. As he reaches Slavin, Slavin with a gesture of his hand stops him.

Slavin: "Nobody else comin'?"

Chambers shakes his head.

Slavin: "Well then, maybe you're right. Maybe Slattery and my boys and me would just be committin' suicide."

Chambers: "That's the way I see it."

Slavin: "I'd be willin' to take that chance, Sheriff, if you and the others felt like I do, that this is a dirty deal, that Hygatt's a thief, and that eventually we're going to have to shoot him out of what he's stolen."

Chambers: "I don't think it will come to that."

Slavin: "Sheriff, you're too old to be wearin' that star. You're not only lettin' this boy down, but you're lettin' down every rancher for miles around—that's the way I see it."

He beckons to his sons and walks away from Chambers. Slavin and his sons mount their horses. Slavin motions with his head, and he and his boys ride off.

Inside the house Chuck has crossed to the window and looks out to see Slavin and his sons leaving. Chuck turns bitterly to Pearl: "That makes the score perfect. I sent my riders away last night." Then with a nod in the direction of Slavin: "And they're movin' out now—that leaves old Peterson, who figures that prayin' will keep Hygatt out of my ranch, and me."

Pearl, softly: "And me."

Chuck, looking at her warily: "How do you mean?"

Pearl: "I think you've got every right to stay and fight. A lot of the men around here ought to envy your courage."

Chuck, a little nervously: "You better be goin'—now."

Pearl: "No. I'm going to stay with you, Chuck. I can help you load."

Suddenly she starts moving around making observations and giving instructions. "I think we ought to put a few buckets of water in here in case a fire should start, ought to barricade the doors, and cover up most of the windows. Get all the food you've got and put it into this one room. If you've got any other rifles let's load them— and we'd better get busy molding some bullets."

Chuck watches her carefully as she moves from the table to the bench, to the window, and suddenly he crosses to her, takes her arm, and turns her around: "It won't work, Pearl."

Pearl looks at him non-committally.

Chuck: "It's kind of a smart trick, figurin' that I wouldn't want to see you get hurt." He shakes his head. "But it won't work. You'll get out of here if I have to have Pete strap you to a horse and take you out."

He crosses to the door, his face angry. Pearl is upset that the scheme hasn't worked.

Chuck: "In some ways, Pearl, what you tried is a dirty trick because you was takin' advantage of somethin' that I feel for you—but you don't feel for me."

Pearl walks up to Chuck and stands close to him: "It was cheap of me." She steps closer to Chuck and puts her hands on his chest. "I was play-acting and that was cheap, but looking at you now and being here makes me know something I never knew before. I don't want you dead, Chuck. Believe that."

Chuck, softly: "I want to believe it."

Pearl: "I know that everything you feel is right. I know the decent people shouldn't have walked out on you, and I know that above all, Chuck, right now I want to stay here with you, no matter what you decide to do." She smiles up at him. "Maybe I won't feel that way when the troubles starts—but, Chuck, I want to be with you."

Chuck looks at Pearl intently. Then with a bit of doubt he turns away and walks out of the house. He goes over to a rose patch that borders the side porch. Pearl follows him out and then crosses over to where Chuck stands, looking down at the roses. As Pearl comes to him, Chuck looks up at her for a moment: "I want to believe everything you said."

Pearl: "Tell me—what are the things you want to fight for?"

Chuck hesitates a moment, then slowly looks around the ranch: "I never put it in words before—maybe I won't be able to tell you. It isn't just the land. It's what's in the land and what the land stands for. The work and the sweat. All the little things like the trees that were planted when they were saplings, places where I used to ride with my father. Every place I look has got a—a memory." Then he looks down at the roses.

Pearl, softly: "That's the kind of immortality anybody can understand."

Chuck looks up at her, and then his fingers indicate the flowers: "There's not much room for flowers on a cow ranch, and yet my mother found time to take care of them. And I watched them ever since she died. Mainly because so much of her went into the growin' of them." He looks up again at Pearl, gently.

Pearl: "Those things *are* worth dying for."

Chuck: "They are if there's nothin' left worth livin' for." He takes a step toward her and takes her hands in his, heatedly: "Are you playin' more games with me, or do you really feel what I do?"

Pearl: "I'm not playing games, Chuck." Then slowly her eyes and lips move toward him: "I'm not playing games."

Chuck searches for the truth, finds it. He takes her in his arms.

Hygatt, Gerrett, Gribbles, Mullison, and five riders pulling a wagon come up toward the Slattery ranch. They are all heavily armed.

Hygatt and his group come to a halt. They are ready for action if there's to be any. They look intently toward the house.

In front of the house Chuck and Pearl have loaded Chuck's wagon with some of his personal effects. Chuck's horse and Pearl's horse are tied to the back of the wagon. Chuck is helping Pearl up to the front seat. As he crosses to get in the other side, Hygatt calls out: "Glad to see you're bein' sensible, Chuck."

Chuck doesn't answer Hygatt, but he looks toward the rear of the house in the direction of the church.

Chuck, calling out: "Are you comin', Pete?"

Peterson's saddled horse stands in front of the church. Peterson, however, stands on the steps of the church, his hat in his hands.

Peterson, calling back: "I'll be along later."

Chuck flicks the reins, and the team starts pulling the wagon. Chuck and Pearl move toward Hygatt and his group in the wagon.

Hygatt: "Good mornin', Miss Saunders."

Pearl doesn't answer. Slowly the wagon passes

Hygatt's group, Pearl and Chuck looking straight ahead.

Gribbles, derisively: "You sure you took everything you needed, Mr. Slattery?"

Chuck works the muscles of his jaw. Pearl reassuringly pats his arm. They continue looking straight ahead.

Hygatt beckons his group in. They ride on to Chuck's grounds.

Chuck looks back in the direction of his ranch.

Hygatt's mob infests his place. The hoofs of the horses of some of Hygatt's riders trample the flower bed.

Chuck's face muscles are working.

Pearl, to Chuck: "Don't, darling—let's look ahead."

Chuck looks at her a moment, nods, turns front and whips the horses. The wagon, picking up speed, rolls up the road.

In front of the church, Hygatt, Gribbles, and Mullison walk up toward where Peterson stands.

Gribbles: "This is somethin' Mr. Slattery forgot to take with him."

Gribbles puts his foot on the step.

Peterson: "You're trespassin' on the house of the Lord."

Hygatt pushes Gribbles to one side and stands looking up at Peterson.

Hygatt: "Now look, Grandpa, I want you to take your cow pony and your prayer book and scoot out of here."

Peterson: "I'll move when the Lord tells me to."

Hygatt nods mock-impressed and turns to Mullison and his men.

Hygatt, sardonically and sarcastically: "Well, boys, it looks as though we'll just have to set around and wait for the Lord to tell old man Peterson when we can take over his church and turn it into a nice cowshed."

Peterson: "May the Lord forgive your blasphemous tongue."

Hygatt: "Seems to me you're askin' the Lord to do a lot of things today." He takes out a gun. "Let's be practical, Peterson. Your Lord is off in the sky somewhere—leastways that's what you claim, and he ain't got a gun. Now I'm right here and I got a gun—and I'm tellin' you to get goin' because I'm comin' in."

Peterson, slowly: "The only way you'll get into this House of God—is over my dead body."

Hygatt, leveling his gun: "Just as you say,

brother." He fires twice in rapid succession. Peterson sinks to the steps dead. Mullison, frightened, quickly and almost surreptitiously crosses himself.

Hygatt steps over the dead body of Peterson and smashes open the doors to the church. He takes a look inside, and then he turns to Gribbles.

Hygatt: "Be as much trouble fixin' it up as buildin' a new one—burn it down—" Then looking at Peterson's body: "And him with it."

Gerrett, Mullison, Gribbles, and two or three of the other men look at the burning church, their faces lighted by the flickering flames. The charred embers of the little church collapse.

On Hygatt's face is the excited fanatical look that he always gets at his moments of triumph. He looks over at Mullison with a hard smile.

Hygatt: "Ever since I was a kid—I loved to watch a fire."

Mullison looks at him, nodding.

◉

    Preparatory to building whatever Hygatt has in mind, a couple of workmen are cleaning up the remains of the cold, black ruins of what once was Peterson's church. Standing looking at the ruins is Chambers. Next to him is his horse. Chambers walks up to the ruins. One of the workmen watches him. His boots scuff some of the ashes.

    Workman: "Lookin' for somethin', Sheriff?"

    Chambers looks at him, shakes his head. The workman turns to continue his work. Chambers takes one or two steps and suddenly stops, looks down. Among some ashes there is a glint of a misshapen piece of metal. Chambers' hand picks up the metal. He straightens up, looking at it intently. It is the coin that Peterson sent for.

    Hygatt: "Mornin', Sheriff."

    Chambers closes his hand around the piece of metal, and as he turns he digs his hand with the coin into his pocket.

    Hygatt followed by Gribbles has ridden up close to the ruins of the church. Chambers walks over toward him.

    Hygatt: "Somethin' on your mind?"

    Chambers: "I was wonderin' what happened to Peterson. It's been a week since Chuck left here, and nobody's seen the Reverend."

    Hygatt: "Least of all me." Then, leaning forward on the saddle: "And let me tell you somethin', Sheriff. Just after Chuck left Peterson was around the church awhile and then high-tailed it out of here leavin' the whole church burnin'—set fire to it himself."

Chambers: "I wouldn't think the Reverend would do a thing like that."

Hygatt: "Maybe you wouldn't, but ten of us here seen him do it." He points a finger. "That buildin' belonged to me legal and rightful, and I just may decide to sue Chuck Slattery for damage to my property."

Chambers looks up at Hygatt, astonished—too astonished to say anything.

Hygatt, still pointing his finger: "So if you ever see that fellow Peterson, tell him to stay away from me. I'm plenty riled."

Chambers looks up at Hygatt, a sudden and complete feeling of defeat and weariness taking hold of him. He nods without saying a word. Then he walks slowly to his horse, mounts, and without a word rides away.

The two workmen who have been listening cannot repress their chuckles. They begin to laugh. Hygatt looks at them with a smile, and then he begins to laugh. Gribbles, who has ridden in with Hygatt, joins in the laughter.

Chambers, wooden-faced, broken, shudders a bit as he hears the laughter and then continues on.

Peterson's coin lies on the counter in Saunders' store. Saunders' fingers are touching the coin. Saunders, Chuck, Chancel, and Chambers are present.

Saunders: "There's no doubt about it, Chuck. That's the coin that Peterson bought."

Chambers, with a sigh: "I believe you, 'Lysses. Chuck, too."

Chancel: "Well, there you are, Ned. That's murder number two though there ain't any way of provin' either one."

Chuck: "It's enough proof for me."

Chancel: "I hate him, Chuck. I think he's a lyin', murderin' thief. Inside me I know that he killed Gorman and Peterson, but he's smart and you can't get a posse together to string up Hygatt just on my not likin' him."

Saunders: "You make sense, Wally. Peterson might of dropped his coin, and, as far as his not bein' around is concerned, it's likely Pete did burn down the church, and he might've wandered off in the hills someplace—Lord knows that we run across the bones of some poor devil years after he's been missin'. How'd you feel if you string up Hygatt and then found out some months later that Peterson was still around?"

Chancel: "Well, speakin' for myself, I wouldn't feel bad at all—"

Chambers: "We should've done somethin' before—leastways I should have. When they first come here there was just the three of them, Hygatt, Gerrett, and Gribbles. And now Mullison is in with them. He's got a crowd of riders out there." He shakes his head miserably. "All my guesses have been wrong."

Just then there is a clap of thunder. Saunders, Chuck, and Chancel peer outside. Chambers is motionless. There is another clap of thunder and a flash of lightning, and the lighting dims down as the oncoming storm darkens the sky.

Saunders, changing the subject from what the men had been talking about: "There's gonna be a heap of rain." He looks at Chambers and puts a hand on Chambers' shoulder. "It ain't the end of the world, Ned, just a summer rain."

Chambers looks at Saunders and turns and goes out of the store, Chancel, Chuck, and Saunders watching him.

It has begun to rain. Chambers, unheeding, walks slowly to the edge of Homeville and up the slope to the cemetery. The rain is soaking him thoroughly. His eyes look in the direction of a grave, and he walks toward it.

The marker on the grave, like the others, is wooden, and the carving on this one reads, "Matthew Slattery, Born 1817, Died 1866." Chambers stands looking at it, and then, oblivious of the rain, he takes off his hat.

Chambers, his voice low: "Matt, I come to tell you I'm sorry. I broke my word to watch out after your boy. I did it because I didn't want there to be any more killin'. I was figurin' that people would want to live in law and order. I was wrong, Matt." His voice breaks a little, and his face is tired as the rain beats down his hair and his head. "And I'm too old, and there's not enough spirit left in me to fix up the bad job I done. Forgive me, Matt. God forgive me."

Chambers turns away, not even thinking to put back his hat. He walks away from the grave and toward Homeville, the rain beating down and soaking into him.

Moon Creek is now in much better repair. One or two new buildings are up. The other buildings are all freshly painted. The street has wooden sidewalks. A saloon is a new and spacious addition, and a few girls have been imported to take care of the men in their free hours.

The entrance to the mine has been widened. A large sign over the mine pit reads, "No. 1 Pit—Two Axes Mining Co." There is increased activity and business in Moon Creek.

Hygatt's office is in first-class condition now. The map is still on the wall. Mullison is seated at a desk, the expression on his face one of concern. Gribbles sits on the window sill, and Gerrett stands leaning against a wall. Hygatt is in front of Mullison.

Mullison: "Sure, I know all about that, but so far we been puttin' out a lot of money and nothin' comes in." Then with a flash of impatience: "And

I'd like to point out that it's been my money." He gets up. "Even the furniture here we got from my place."

Hygatt, slowly: "You don't think you've gone in over your head, do you, Bunny?"

Mullison: "Look, I don't like to be talked to that way."

Gerrett straightens up, anticipating trouble. Mullison looks first at Gerrett, then Hygatt, then Gribbles, who has also moved a little from his perch on the window sill.

Mullison, his voice calm: "All I'm sayin' is that you still haven't made the deal with the railroad. We're beginnin' to pile up a lot of coal—where's it goin'?" Then a little helplessly: "That's all I'm askin'."

Hygatt: "I'm leavin' for Omaha next week to make the deal." He points his finger at some letters which are on the desk. "Read the letters again, Bunny. It's a deal. All I got to do is sign it."

Mullison, a little petulantly: "I think I ought to go to Omaha with you and look over the deal."

Hygatt: "I don't think you'll be needed, Bunny."

Just then the door is opened quickly, and they all turn, surprised. Standing in the door is Al Yunker. Yunker is a tall, slim, well-built man. Under a short-crowned hat we catch glimpses of his completely bald head. Yunker carries himself with the ease and assurance of a man who knows that he is a deadly killer. He carries a double-barrelled, sawed-off shotgun, and around his hips he wears two cartridge belts with holsters that carry two forty-four revolvers. He stands in the doorway and looks at the men in the room.

His eyes still on the men, Yunker takes a step in, reaches back with his free hand, and closes the door behind him.

Yunker: "Howdy."

Hygatt nods.

Mullison, almost agasp: "Al Yunker!"

Yunker, looking at Mullison: "That's right—Al Yunker. I didn't get your name."

Mullison: "Bunny Mullison."

Yunker nods and looks at Hygatt.

Yunker: "You're Hygatt."

Hygatt nods.

Yunker: "I've heard about you. I used to kill a man and take his money and his boots—you've got a new twist. You take his land—you got somethin' to show for it."

Hygatt, graciously: "I always thought it a shame that a man with your talent was forced out of this territory."

Yunker: "I came back to take a look around." Then slowly: "You're gonna need men."

Hygatt: "Are there enough of your fellows around for any practical use?"

Yunker nods: "I can get enough. With horses and guns—" Then with a grim smile: "And like you said—talent."

Hygatt: "All right, bring 'em in. I'll have quarters for you."

Yunker: "Fine. We'll talk over other details when I get back."

He lifts his hand in a little flat salute.

Yunker: "Here's to prosperity."

Then just as quickly and as dramatically as he came in, he turns and goes out.

Mullison has seated himself during Yunker's talk with Hygatt. Now Mullison jumps up quickly. He crosses to Hygatt.

Mullison: "Are you crazy?"

Hygatt's face freezes.

Mullison: "There's a price on Yunker. Everybody'll know about his being here—they'll know about us."

Hygatt, his face hard: "Let 'em know—there's a time when a man has to make his owns laws and his own rules." He takes a close step toward Bunny. "I'm makin' my rules from now in, and you're living by 'em—or if you want—dyin' by them."

The grim look on Hygatt's face frightens Mullison. His jaw develops a bit of slack.

Mullison, hoarsely: "You're not talking like a man in his right mind."

Hygatt puts his hand on Bunny's chest and then gives Bunny a little shove backward.

Hygatt: "Sit down."

Bunny bites nervously on his lips and sits down. Hygatt, with murderous calm, leans down toward Mullison.

Hygatt: "You may as well understand a lot of things. From here in, I run the show like I want, and if I say Yunker's in—Yunker's in."

For a moment it looks as though Bunny is going to accept this challenge.

Hygatt, taking a half step backward and eyeing Mullison: "I think you're tagged, Bunny. If I was to slap you across the face, I don't think you'd have enough guts to reach for your gun."

And with that he takes the back of his left hand and slaps it across Mullison's mouth, and then he stands poised, his right hand ready to reach for his gun. Mullison swallows hard, his face sweaty.

Hygatt: "That's how I figured. Now from here in, behave."

Mullison rubs his hand over his lips again, looks helplessly up to Hygatt, and shakes his head.

Mullison, hoarsely: "There ain't no sense in losing your temper." He tries a sick smile. Hygatt, deliberately turning his back, walks away. He crosses to the map, his finger again traces the Living Valley that they now control.

Hygatt: "I think we're about ready to talk

business with Mr. Poling." His finger illustrates his next move. "And after him Franson and then Slavin." He makes a gesture. "That's all for the time being." He points his finger at Poling's ranch. "You agree about us first seein' Mr. Poling."

Bunny nods helplessly. Hygatt smiles at Gerrett who is looking at Bunny with contempt.

Hygatt, Mullison, Gerrett, Gribbles, and Poling are riding together. Poling is in a very expansive mood. His left hand grips the reins of the horse, and his right hand is making extravagant gestures as he rides. Hygatt rides closest to Poling and feeds Poling's exuberance.

Poling: "It's all yours now, Hygatt—all the scrubby, dirty, treeless acres—all yours." He turns in his saddle and looks at Mullison. "Yours, too, Mr. Mullison."

Mullison nods.

Poling: "And when you're ridin' the range, sweatin' the dust out of your lungs, think of me off in Oregon with a fruit ranch and green hills and great big fir trees and the damp of the sea in my hair—that's livin'—and twenty thousand dollars of your money in my jeans."

Hygatt: "I'm glad it worked out so nice, Poling—a fine deal for you and for us."

Poling: "My line runs up to the clump of cottonwoods—right along the creek—" He looks at Hygatt and smiles. "Mostly dry." His hand has described an arc from the cottonwoods and is now at the left side of the arc. He continues, his eyes following his hand. "All the way down to the foothills."

By now the men have reached a point where they can see in the distance a group of people working on a very crude shed. The upright timbers are in place, and four or five men working, busily employed hammering some other uprights into place.

Hygatt looks off at them. Poling also becomes aware of them.

Hygatt: "Are those your men?"

Poling: "No, I paid off my boys this morning like you told me to."

Hygatt keeps staring out in the direction of the men. Poling decides to give an explanation: "That's my new neighbor." He turns to Hygatt, bows in his saddle. "*Your* new neighbor—Mr. Slavin."

Hygatt: "I think we ought to tell Mr. Slavin the good news."

Poling nods. They spur their horses and start toward Slavin.

The men are Slavin and four of his sons. They are in work clothes, sweaty, dirty. Their attention has been attracted to Hygatt and the others as they ride up toward them. Slavin takes a look and then looks back at his sons.

Slavin: "Ain't you ever seen a horse? Keep workin'."

The boys go back to their labors. Slavin stands waiting, a hammer in his hand as Hygatt, Poling, and the others ride up.

Poling: "Greetings, neighbor."

Slavin nods and then waits for the others to speak. He puts the hammer on a rough work bench and fusses with his pipe and tobacco.

Poling: "Well, I'm gonna be leavin' yuh." This information is no bolt of thunder to Slavin. "Mr. Hygatt and Mr. Mullison are takin' over —and I'm jes' showin' 'em the boundaries."

Again Slavin nods.

Hygatt: "There's no reason, Slavin, why we can't be good neighbors."

Slavin, shortly: "No reason."

Hygatt: "And in time maybe all the neighbors can cooperate for the good of the territory."

Slavin: "I'm for that."

Hygatt: "Good idea your puttin' your cattle shelter down here in this hollow. Fact, I think I'll put one in for myself right next to it."

Hygatt's gesture indicates that he intends to build the shed on Slavin's side of the dry creek.

Slavin has finished packing his pipe. He takes a

step forward: "My line runs along this dry creek. You can do anything you want on the land up to the creek, but if one post or one shed or one foot comes a quarter of an inch over that line—" He looks up at Hygatt.

Hygatt nods with a hard smile on his face: "I figure you're the kind of man that would stand up for his rights. Mr. Slavin—we'll get along fine."

Slavin picks up his hammer, clenches the pipe between his teeth.

Slavin, through his teeth to Poling: "Good luck to you, Mr. Poling." He turns and resumes his work.

Hygatt, Poling, and the others spur their horses and move away.

Poling is standing in front of the counter in Saunders' store. From a money bag he has taken some coins and is letting them drop on the counter in front of Saunders, who is behind the counter. Chancel and Pearl are to one side watching. Pearl holds a bottle of liniment and some white cloths.

Franson is sitting up on the counter looking at Poling.

Poling, as the coins drop: "Say when, 'Lysses."

'Lysses makes a gesture for Poling to stop. He picks up some of the money and leaves the rest on the counter.

Saunders: "It's all you owe me. The rest is yours."

Poling, putting the coins back in his pocket: "There's plenty left over for a couple of rounds at the Blackjack—all on me." He makes a gesture. "Goodbye from Mr. Poling to his neighbors."

Chancel: "When do you plan to leave?"

Poling: "Leavin' sunrise tomorrow morning. Want to be over the Divide before winter, and every hour brings me closer to Oregon."

Franson: "Takin' all that hard cash with you?"

Poling: "Every cent of it—worked thirty-two years, and everything I worked for I got my hands on. I'm gonna keep my hands on it—probably catch up with a wagon train outside of Virginia City—" He makes a little salute. "And Westward Ho!"

Chancel: "When did you close this deal with Hygatt?"

Poling: "Yesterday. Nicest man to deal with I ever seen—and I don't mind sayin' I think I was a little wrong about Bunny Mullison too—didn't argue with me about price. I told them what I wanted, and they paid it right on the nail."

Saunders, to Chancel: "See, Wally, like I told you, Hygatt paid for everything he's gotten here—and it ran to a lot of money these last few weeks. Far as I'm concerned, he keeps his promises."

Pearl, to Wally: "I'd better get over to see Mr. Chambers." She looks at Poling. "The best of everything to you, Mr. Poling."

Poling: "Thank you. Say good-by to the sheriff for me, and I hope he gets over the misery he's got." He extends his hand to Chancel. "So long, Wally."

Chancel: "Good-by and good luck." Then to Franson: "Might be a good idea to keep Poling company." He smiles at Poling. "You're going to do a little celebratin', and it might be a good idea to keep someone around to see you get off all right tomorrow morning."

Franson nods seriously, getting exactly what Chancel means: "Sure, Wally—that's a good idea."

Chancel and Pearl leave the store.

Poling, to Saunders: "Come on, 'Lysses. Close up the place and join me in a libation."

Saunders: "Might not be a bad idea!"

Poling and Franson ride up to Poling's house and dismount. The house is a simple bachelor's shack. Poling is very happily drunk. He is singing in a loud voice a song called "I'm Bound Away for the Wild Missouri." He staggers heavily, and Franson supports him as they walk toward the house.

Standing in the deep shadow under the porch are Yunker, Gribbles, Hygatt, and Mullison.

Poling continues his song in a screeching voice.

Yunker, whispering: "You figured he was goin' to be alone."

Hygatt: "It's all right. We can take care of Franson at the same time—two for one."

Franson, supporting the staggering Poling, approaches the house. From out of the shadows under the porch into the dim moonlight step the figures of the men waiting. Mullison moves to one side of the porch.

Poling, not frightened: "Hullo! Hullo, boys! Good evenin'!"

Franson with his left hand still supports Poling. His right hand hangs near his gun ready for action.

Hygatt: "Evenin', Poling." Then with a little smile: "Didn't spend all your money, did you?"

Poling, exhibiting sacks of money in his left hand: "'s all here! Minus only three hundred and twenty dollars—everybody have a drink!"

Gribbles looks over at Hygatt. Hygatt nods. Gribbles quickly takes out his gun. Yunker steps up holding a shot gun.

Poling: "What's goin' on? What you doin'—you tryin' to steal my money?" He turns to Franson. "L-le-let's get out of here!"

Hygatt: "Don't get frightened. We've just come to say good-by."

With that he takes out his gun, and he and Gribbles shoot. Poling twists about crazily. Yunker now fires his gun into Poling who falls dead. Franson bravely, though hopelessly, goes for his gun. Gribbles shoots the gun out of Franson's hand. Mullison takes a knife from a sheath in his belt and flings it. The knife sinks into Franson's back. He contracts his shoulders, turns, and sinks to the ground.

Hygatt looks at Mullison. "Nice, Bunny. You're handy with that." Mullison is a little proud.

Yunker and Gribbles stand over the dead body of Poling and the wounded figure of Franson.

Gribbles, to Hygatt, his gun pointing at Franson: "Finish him off?"

Hygatt, shaking his head: "No. Let's take him home." Now as he gets his idea, he comes down toward Gribbles. "The man's been hurt—the least we can do is bring him home." He looks at Gribbles. "Tsk, tsk. I'm ashamed of you, Gribbles." He smiles and looks down at Franson. He beckons to Gribbles and Yunker as they bend down to pick up Franson.

The interior of the Franson ranch house is very well—ordered, neat, and clean. The furniture undoubtedly was brought out from New England, and the place is kept spick and span by Mrs. Franson.

This night Mrs. Franson, aroused from her sleep, is standing in the room near a table on which an oil lamp is burning. She has a frightened look on her face. Hygatt stands at the door with Mullison.

Hygatt: "Nothin' to be frightened about, Mrs. Franson. Your husband's going to be all right."

Mrs. Franson, dazed, shakes her head a bit as Gerrett and Gribbles carry Franson into the room. Mrs. Franson sees her husband, and she rushes toward him.

Mrs. Franson: "Jack—Jack, what's happened to you—Jack, darling!"

Gerrett and Gribbles carry Franson toward a door.

Gerrett, looking at Mrs. Franson: "Where's the bed?"

Mrs. Franson frantically indicates the next room. As they start into the bedroom, Hygatt crosses to the table, picks up the oil lamp, and goes into the bedroom.

In the dark room Gerrett and Gribbles, carrying Franson, walk toward the bed. Hygatt and Mullison enter, holding the lamp which illuminates the room. Mrs. Franson kneels down beside her husband.

Mrs. Franson: "Jack, please, dear—"

Hygatt, stepping closer toward the bed: "He had an accident."

Mrs. Franson looks up at Hygatt and then looks back at her husband.

Franson, turning his head and gaining hold of his consciousness: "They killed Poling—knifed me—"

Mrs. Franson touches her husband's wounded hand uneasily. Hygatt and the others just look down without a word.

Franson, continuing: "—in the back."

Mrs. Franson helps her husband turn over on his stomach. She sees the dark stain of blood on his shirt. She puts her hand to her mouth to gasp, then frantically she looks up at Hygatt.

Mrs. Franson: "Help me, please help me! He'll die."

Hygatt: "Of course we'll help you." He looks

at Gerrett. "Get the lady some water—some towels."

Mrs. Franson: "In the kitchen."

Gerrett clumps noisily out of the room.

Franson, turning his head and looking at his wife: "They killed Poling—shot him down like an animal."

Mrs. Franson: "Who? Tell me. Who did it? Who did this to you?"

Franson, looking at Hygatt and Mullison: "They did."

Mrs. Franson looks up at Hygatt again.

Hygatt, with a little nod of his head: "I'll tell you just what happened, Mrs. Franson—and you listen, too, Brother Franson, because this is just what happened." He takes a step forward. "Mr. Franson brought Mr. Poling home and said goodby to Poling who left for Oregon. Mr. Franson came here and had an accident and cut his back very, very badly, and we're gonna stay here to help you run things while Mr. Franson's sick. Some of our men who're helping us dig coal are gonna stay here, and we've made an arrangement for you to see that they're well fed and taken care of in exchange for workin' your ranch and developing your coal pit.

Mrs. Franson, bewildered and shaking her head: "I don't know what you're sayin'." She turns to her husband.

Hygatt leans down, puts his hand on Mrs. Franson's robe and pulls her up.

Hygatt, shaking her with his hand: "I'll tell it to you a couple more times before morning, and you gotta remember that's what happened because if you don't, your husband'll never get off that bed and you're liable to have an accident—fatal."

Gerrett returns with a pan of water and some cloths.

Hygatt, his manner changing: "You know, Mrs. Franson, you ought to do something about fixin' up your husband's back."

Mrs. Franson, intimidated, bewildered, soaks a cloth in the water and then bends to her knees again and starts to pull her husband's shirt and fix up his back.

Mr. and Mrs. Franson look at each other.

Franson: "Do just as they say, Anna."

Mrs. Franson nods her head, and as she begins working on Mr. Franson's back, he winces in pain. Hygatt and the others watch Mrs. Franson take care of her husband.

Hygatt, to Gribbles: "You, boy, better plan on stayin' here, and I'll send over four or five others to help out. You pay off Franson's men in the morning and send them riding." Then with a hard smile: "And I want you to be very attentive to Mr. and Mrs. Franson. Take care of their every want and never let them out of your sight." Gribbles nods, and Hygatt turns to Mullison. "Bunny, it's been a long night." He turns and walks out followed by Mullison.

Gerrett and Gribbles stand looking down at Mrs. Franson. She stops a moment and looks up at Gribbles: "Why do you do this to us?"

Gribbles shrugs, considers the question a moment, then smiles as he gets the answer: "You see, Mrs. Franson, you just happened to get in the way of progress."

Gerrett, leaning against the wall as he watches: "Lady, you can't make an omelet without breaking eggs."

Gribbles nods at Gerrett. Mrs. Franson returns her attention to her husband and bows her head, sobbing.

Chuck is driving a freight wagon pulled by four horses. Hitched to the back of Chuck's wagon is an unsaddled, painted cow pony. Sitting next to Chuck on the front seat is a husky, bearded man named Belger. Belger carries a rifle across his knees. The wagon is headed toward Franson's ranch house.

Two or three men loll around the front of the Franson house. Gerrett and Gribbles, unseen by Chuck and Belger, are sitting on a low hillock near the house facing a headstone to one side of the house. Chuck is looking off with interest at the Franson house and the people grouped in front of it. He drives his wagon to the front of the house.

Chuck, calling out as he gets off: "Jack—Mrs. Franson."

He crosses to the back of the wagon, looks at the painted cow pony a moment, slaps it affectionately on the flank, and then continues up to the house. He looks at the men, who eye him, and then suddenly Chuck stops, seeing Gerrett and Gribbles for the first time. They each idly twirl a revolver.

Gribbles: "Hello." He then turns, looks at Gerrett. "There's our friend, Mr. Slattery. He's got himself a nice job."

Gerrett and Gribbles watch as Chuck walks to the front of the house.

Chuck: "Mrs. Franson."

Gribbles gets up at this point and saunters over to the front porch and leans against the rail. Then he calls inside to the house: "Mrs. Franson!"

Chuck looks at Gribbles, and then Mrs. Franson comes out of the house. She stands there.

Mrs. Franson: "Hello, Chuck."

Chuck, flicking the brim of his hat: "Hello. Jack around?"

Mrs. Franson's voice is wooden. She speaks dully and slowly as if having carefully rehearsed all the false facts that Hygatt gave her. As she talks, Gribbles eyes her: "Jack's sick. He hurt himself. He cut his back. He can't see anybody."

Chuck: "When did that happen?"

Mrs. Franson, in the same automaton manner: "Poling sold his ranch and went West. Jack took him home, and comin' back he had a fall."

Chuck: "Is there anything the matter? You seem tired. Can I help?"

Mrs. Franson: "Don't want to see anybody."

Chuck looks at Gribbles, who takes his eyes off Mrs. Franson to smile crookedly at Chuck.

Chuck, looking back at Mrs. Franson: "I picked up a painted pony that Jack wanted me to find."

Mrs. Franson: "Just tie it in the stable."

Chuck: "Could I see Jack a minute?"

Mrs. Franson: "He can't see anybody—just tie the pony in the stable." And with that she turns and walks back into the house.

Chuck takes a half step to follow Mrs. Franson, but Gribbles holds his gun in a half-threatening position.

Gribbles: "She don't feel good, and she don't want to see nobody."

Chuck turns. He crosses to the wagon, unties the pony and starts back to the rear of the house.

Gribbles walks to a position where he can watch Chuck leading the pony to the stable. As Chuck leads the pony in, his eyes flash around. They narrow as he sees something. Some men are digging into the side of one of the hillocks of Franson's place. He finishes placing the pony in the stable, walks back, and meets Gribbles.

Chuck: "What's goin' on here?"

Gribbles: "Well, you see Mr. Franson has gone into the coal mining business, and he hired some of us to help him out. His own riders are looking for work someplace else."

Chuck takes this in and nods.

At one of the windows of the house, Mrs. Franson stands looking out, her face distraught and unhappy.

Chuck comes up to the wagon and gets into the seat beside Belger. Gribbles watches them go. As the wagon starts to pull away, Gribbles rejoins Gerrett on the hillock.

Mrs. Franson comes out of the house suddenly.

Mrs. Franson, almost a whisper: "Chuck!"

Gribbles turns quickly and looks back at Mrs. Franson.

Gribbles: "Shut up!"

As he turns back, he carefully aims his revolver at the headstone and fires. The headstone is on a small grave. There is carved on it in rude homemade lettering:

Leon Franson
Died 1871—Aged One Year

Gribbles' bullet chips the headstone. Now Gerrett fires at the headstone, then Gribbles, then Gerrett. Mrs. Franson grabs at her chest and closes her eyes in desperation.

Chuck and Belger on the wagon hear the sound of the shooting. Belger is in a position where he can look out the side of the wagon and see what's happening.

Chuck: "What is it?"

Belger: "Just some target shootin', I guess."

Chuck nods his head slowly, and, as Belger straightens up and leans against the side of the wagon, Chuck continues driving the team without saying a word.

In the bedroom of Chambers' home, Chambers is stretched out in bed. His wife sits on a chair near him, her head in her hands. Wally Chancel stands at the foot of the bed. Pearl is wiping the perspiration from Chambers' face with a cloth. Saunders stands near the bed looking down at him when Chambers opens his eyes.

Saunders, softly to Chambers: "That's it, Ned."

Chambers, his voice weak: "Glad you're here, 'Lysses—Wally—"

Mrs. Chambers lowers her hands, reaches over, and takes one of her husband's hands in hers. Just then there is the sound of a door opening. Pearl looks in the direction of the sound.

Chuck enters Chambers' room softly and crosses toward the bed. He nods at the others, but doesn't say anything.

Chambers, talking while Chuck comes in: "Not gettin' over this, 'Lysses."

Chancel: "Sure you will."

Chambers, briefly: "'Lysses, make sure that Wally takes over. Make sure—" Slowly he turns his head and looks at his wife.

Mrs. Chambers: "I'm here, Ned."

Chambers slowly nods, then closes his eyes, and falls into his final sleep. His passing is so quiet and so natural that for a moment no one realizes it, but suddenly Mrs. Chambers feels Chambers' hand. She looks up helplessly at Pearl. Pearl glances over in the direction of Chancel, who comes closer to the bed and puts his hand on Chambers' heart. He looks at Saunders. Saunders takes Mrs. Chambers by the arm and helps her from the chair.

Saunders: "There's nothing you can do for him."

Pearl goes to Chuck, who puts his arm around her, and they both stand looking down at Chambers' body as Chancel completes his examination and then covers the dead man's face with a blanket.

A group of perhaps twenty men has gathered in Saunders' store. Quist is one of them. Saunders stands near the counter, Chancel next to him. Chuck is sitting on the edge of the counter. Saunders tells Chancel: "Wally, you hear the votin'. You're Sheriff by unanimous choice."

Wally nods at Saunders and turns to the others: "Men, I hope I can do a good job. I think we're runnin' into some troubled times. I'm liable to need help, and I hope I get it."

He waves a little salute of thanks at the men. Quist sidles over and slaps Chancel on the back.

Quist: "Every man Jack of us is with ya."

Wally looks at Quist and nods, not impressed. The meeting, without anyone formally announcing it, is over. The men get up, and a couple of them come over and shake hands with Wally, one or two slap him on the arm, and they meander out. The store is empty now except for Chancel, Chuck, and Saunders.

Saunders: "Wally, come up and eat with us this noon."

Chancel: "Thanks."

Chuck: "I'm glad you're Sheriff, Wally. You know—" He looks at the two men. "I gotta say what I feel. I'm sorry that a man named Ned Chambers is dead. But I'm hoping that a lot of things Ned Chambers stood for died with him."

Saunders looks at Chuck.

Chuck: "They're a couple of things in my mind—"

Saunders: "Let it wait, Chuck. Pearl's upstairs puttin' dinner on the table. Come on."

Chuck agrees wordlessly, and they start out of the store.

◎

Saunders' living room is arranged for twelve o'clock dinner. At the table are seated Chuck, Chancel, Saunders, and Pearl.

Saunders, helping himself to another piece of pie: "Well, it may be likely. After all, Mullison went into business with Hygatt. Maybe there is coal there. Maybe Franson *is* sick."

Chuck, testily: "Maybe this—maybe that. But I know Anna Franson. She was sayin' one thing to me and meanin' another."

Chancel: "I think I'll ride over and have a look around."

Saunders: "Strikes me you can save yourself a lot of horseflesh."

Chuck, leaning forward: "Mr. Saunders, how long does it take you to learn? *I* know that Hygatt cheated me out of my place. *I* know he killed Gorman and Peterson. *I* know that I didn't pass Poling on the road he was supposed to be takin'.

I know that Hygatt killed Poling and has probably taken over Franson's place."

Saunders: "You don't know nothin', Chuck. If you or Wally could once show me that you know—know in the sense of it being fact—then maybe I'd listen. But up to now the only fact I do know is that everything Hygatt's done has been legal."

Chancel: "Ned Chambers was an honorable man, and he figured that everybody else was. And Ulysses, you think because you run a business that everybody who pays his bills on time is a decent man."

Chuck: "I lived on my place from the time my father died. I worked it, built it, believing that if I got in trouble there were decent people around who would stand by. They didn't. This whole territory is gettin' stinkin' and rotten with people who are too soft and dumb to fight."

Saunders, his face clouding with anger: "You're pickin' a lot of wrong words to say what you feel, Chuck."

Pearl, rising and speaking for the first time: "Dad—Chuck—you shouldn't be saying these things to each other."

Chuck, rising suddenly: "I'm riding my wagon back to Omaha and when I get there, I'm quittin' and I'll begin all over again." He looks at Pearl. "I wish you'd come with me, Pearl. You belong with me."

Saunders: "I've got something to say about what Pearl does, and Pearl's got something to say for herself."

Chuck, going right through with the challenge: "Then suppose we let Pearl do the talkin'."

There is a beat or two pause.

Chuck: "It'll be an hour before I shove off, Pearl—you make up your mind."

He picks up his hat and starts for the door, turns. Chuck's voice is a little softer as he talks to Pearl: "I want you to come with me. It's our last chance for being happy."

Then he turns and walks out, closing the door behind him. The sound of his walking down the steps can be heard. Slowly, Pearl moves across the room to her father. She takes his hand.

Pearl: "Dad—"

Chancel: "I'll run along, 'Lysses."

Pearl: "No, wait. You can hear this."

Saunders looks at Pearl.

Pearl: "Dad—I'm going with Chuck."

Saunders: "Look, Pearl, this is something you have to think out."

Pearl, shaking her head: "No. You can waste a lot of time thinking things out, and you're liable to lose something awful precious." Then her voice lowers. "I don't want to lose Chuck."

Saunders lowers his head a moment.

Pearl: "I think he's right about a lot of things. I don't know any more than he does about Hygatt, but I am sure that I love Chuck and I want to be with him, no matter what."

Saunders, a little harshly: "Well then, you've only got an hour. You better get ready."

Pearl is about to answer him but changes her mind and walks into the bedroom. Saunders looks up at Chancel.

Chancel thinks this is an opening wedge: "'Lysses, you're the one man in this town people'd listen to. You say the word, and every man will ride in a posse and sweat the truth out of Hygatt and his men. It can't be done by me or a couple of us. It'll need all of us—you can give 'em the word."

Saunders, eyeing Chancel: "Sure I can, but I'm not going to be bullied into actin' against what my reason tells me. And I'm not going to give the word that'll hamstring the territory and make Bloody Kansas look like a pink tea."

Chancel, with a little shrug: "When Chambers died this morning Chuck said that a lot of the things that Chambers stood for died with him. I hate to say this, 'Lysses, but they didn't."

Then slowly Chancel walks to the door, taking his hat, and goes down the steps. Saunders stands there, an isolated, lonely figure. His hands take hold of the edge of the table, and he sways a bit with the weight of the emotional wallops he has received. He is bent and despairing.

Chuck's wagon team stands in front of the Homeville freight office. Belger is carrying some small boxes from the office into the wagon. Chuck is checking the harness. Lolling against the front of the place is Quist. Chuck looks up for a moment in the direction of Saunders' store. There is no activity. He looks back a little disappointed.

Belger, as he comes to the front of the wagon: "We better get movin', Chuck, if you aim to camp at the ford."

Chuck nods. Wally Chancel walks up, followed by Holly, the bartender, and another man who at the moment is just sight-seeing. His name is Hellens.

Chuck, to Chancel, extending his hand: "I don't know when I'll see you again, Wally—or if."

Chancel: "Good luck."

Just then their attention is attracted by the

sound of horses' hoofs and the creak of a wagon. They look up as a small covered wagon pulled by two horses comes up toward Chuck's wagon. Seated in the wagon are Mr. and Mrs. Norton. She is a woman of about forty who looks closer to sixty. Her husband is a very heavily muscled, good-looking, bearded man. As he comes toward Chuck's wagon Norton lifts his hand.

Norton: "Glad you're here, Chuck."

Chuck: "Hello." Nodding: "Mrs. Norton—"

Norton: "We sold out our ranch, and we want to ride with you—"

Mrs. Norton: "Jim says there's safety in numbers."

Chuck: "Glad to have you. How far you goin'?"

Mrs. Norton: "Clear east. When we get to Omaha, get ourselves on a train and back to Ohio."

Chancel: "Sorry to see you leave."

Norton: "Kinda surprise to me, Wally—only yesterday had a call from Mr. Hygatt and Mullison—they bought my place." He nods his head. "Paid a mighty handsome cash price—no bargainin' at all. Seemed mighty generous."

Chancel: "He paid off your riders, didn't he? Told you he was goin' to use his own men?"

Norton, a little surprised: "Yes. How did you know?"

Chancel looks at Chuck. They exchange a knowing glance. Chuck then looks at Norton.

Chuck: "We'll be keepin' each other company to Omaha."

Norton: "With all that hard cash in my wagon I'll appreciate the company."

Quist slowly ambles away from the group, apparently unconcerned.

Norton pulls up the street a bit, then turns his horses around so that he is in line with Chuck's wagon. Chuck fusses with the harness another moment, waves a salute at Chancel, and looks at Saunders' store.

Suddenly out of the store runs Pearl. In back of her walks Saunders holding two carpet bags. Pearl, as she comes out, waves and calls: "Chuck!"

Chuck smiles happily. In back of him, Chancel smiles too. Chuck trots toward Pearl, and as he reaches her they embrace.

Saunders walks up. "That's the way she wants it, Chuck, so—" He pats Chuck's shoulder. "The best to both of you."

Chuck: "Thanks, Mr. Saunders." He puts out his hands for Pearl's carpet bags and takes them from Saunders. He puts the bags in the back of the wagon, and helps Pearl up to the front seat.

Belger, who is standing nearby: "Mighty glad you're comin' along, Miss Saunders. You're a heap prettier thing to look at than Chuck."

Pearl smiles at him. Belger mounts the saddle horse that stands near the wagon, and Chuck gets into the wagon.

Chuck and Pearl look out from the side of the wagon. She waves: "Goodbye, Dad. I'll write often and see you soon."

Saunders puts up his hand and waves his fingers. Chancel waves good-by. Chuck snaps the whip, and the horses start out. His wagon rides down the street, followed by Norton's wagon. Belger is riding at the side.

Saunders puts his hand on Chancel's shoulder, looking at the receding wagons: "I'm going to be mighty lonesome without Pearl."

Chancel turns his head and looks at Saunders: "You'd be a lot less lonely if you was to ride with your neighbors against Hygatt."

Saunders: "I'll ride when I'm ready."

Chancel: "When you're ready to help—I hope it won't be too little and too late." He turns and walks away.

Quist walks up the street on the side opposite Holly's saloon. In front of the saloon stands a tall, scraggly-bearded rider. Quist comes up and leans against the wall near the rider. As Chuck's and Norton's wagons pass in front, Quist mumbles something to the tall rider. Having delivered the message, Quist saunters down the street.

The rider hasn't answered, but immediately

straightens himself, goes to his horse, mounts it, and rides slowly down the street. He puts his horse into a leisurely trot, and then, as he crosses the bridge past the schoolhouse, he heads his horse northeast and breaks into a fast gallop.

◎

The Nortons, Chuck, Belger, and Pearl have made camp for the night near a stream in a clump of cottonwood trees, and have built a fire in the shelter of the wagons. They are all gathered around the fire, Pearl and Chuck sitting close to each other, preoccupied. Belger is sitting near the fire playing the harmonica. Mr. Norton stands just behind where his wife sits looking at Chuck and Pearl. The two couples, listening to Belger play, are concerned at this moment with their thoughts. Belger stops playing and slaps the harmonica against his palm.

Mrs. Norton: "Thank you, Mr. Belger. That was real lovely."

Norton: "We got a lot of ridin' to do tomorrow. I vote we turn in." He lets his hand fall on Mrs. Norton's shoulder, and without another word he turns and walks toward his wagon.

Belger: "Second the motion—good night."

Chuck waves a good night. Belger walks a short distance away to a blanket roll he has fixed up on the ground. Pearl, who has been sitting with a blanket across her shoulders, draws it closer around herself. Chuck notices the movement and wordlessly gets up and puts some more wood on the fire. Then he comes back and sits down next to Pearl, who nods her thanks to him. Mrs. Norton rises from the dead log that she was sitting on and goes over to Chuck and Pearl. The light plays on Mrs. Norton's face.

Mrs. Norton: "May I say something?"

Pearl: "Of course, Mrs. Norton."

Mrs. Norton: "I been sittin' watching you. I know, Miss Saunders, that you've made a sudden decision to go with Chuck."

Chuck nods.

Mrs. Norton, slowly: "It's only natural that you should be asking yourself did you do the right thing. Not because you don't love Chuck but because you don't know whether it's right for him and right for you."

Chuck and Pearl exchange a look and then look up at Mrs. Norton whose voice continues: "I had to make a decision like that too. Nineteen years ago I went with—I went with Mr. Norton like he wanted me to." A nod of her head indicates her husband. "I was young—" She considers a moment. "And pretty—and I liked to dance. And we came out here and we worked the earth. My hands got hard. I had two children—we lost them both." She shakes her head. "We had nothin' but the land and each other. Now Mr. Norton wants to go back to Ohio, and I'm goin' with him." She hesitates a moment. "I mighta stayed in my home town, married somebody else, had a regular house with carpets—" She looks at her hands. "And my hands wouldn't be so rough."

Chuck and Pearl are listening to every word. Chuck is more concerned than Pearl because he feels that perhaps Mrs. Norton is talking Pearl out of going with him.

Mrs. Norton again hesitates and looks down at them. Then she smiles slowly. "But I love Mr. Norton, and I wouldn't have been happy anywhere except with him."

Norton's voice: "Mother, you better turn in."

She looks in the direction of the voice, smiles, and looks back at Chuck and Pearl. Mrs. Norton, slowly: "Every day and night for twenty years —his voice—that's better than a house with carpets. Good night." She walks away toward the wagon.

Pearl is looking at Mrs. Norton. Chuck looks at Pearl. Then slowly Pearl turns and looks at Chuck. He waits. Pearl smiles at him.

Pearl, slowly: "Every day and every night— your voice." She leans toward him, and they embrace.

Out of sight, a group of riders is approaching the campfire—Hygatt, Mullison, Gerrett, Gribbles, Yunker, the lanky rider Quist was talking to, and one other man. They walk their horses slowly. The only sound is the creak of leather and the soft clop-clop of the horses' hoofs. Hygatt lifts his hand in a gesture for them to stop. He dismounts, and the others dismount with him. They walk toward the little camp.

Pearl is now asleep in the wagon. Chuck is asleep in a blanket roll under the wagon. Mr. and Mrs. Norton are asleep in their wagon. Belger is in the blanket roll to one side.

Chuck stirs and slowly opens his eyes. He listens, then rises a bit on his elbow. He hears the faint cracking of a twig. As he slowly pulls the blanket roll off and reaches for his gun, Gerrett looms over him and quickly smashes the butt of his revolver against Chuck's head.

Belger has heard the sound and, startled, jumps up, grabbing at his gun. As they see Belger rise Gribbles and Yunker both fire. The bullets pound into Belger, and he twists and falls dead. These shots, of course, rouse Pearl, Norton, and Mrs. Norton. Norton jumps out of the wagon, his gun in his hand. As he fires, Mullison and Hygatt's guns flash towards Norton. Norton sags against the back of the wagon. His wife appears and takes the gun from his hand. As she turns and shoots toward the sudden, unexpected, and unseen enemy, Gerrett fires at Mrs. Norton. She half drops out of the wagon, her hair falling down. Her dying hand feels for her husband's arm, and then she shudders and dies.

Hygatt's group has now completely entered the camp area, their guns poised, looking for more to kill. Mullison jumps into the Norton wagon and begins to search for the money, striking matches to see his way.

Terror stricken, but determined to get away, Pearl gets out of the front of the wagon. She crosses to where the horses are picketed, disengages one horse, and leaps to its back. As she starts to ride, Hygatt, Gerrett, and Gribbles hear the sound of a horse beginning to move. They look intently.

Hygatt, talking to the others but looking toward the sound: "I think that's Miss Saunders—she's always had bad manners." He lifts his gun, aims, fires.

The horse has been running, but as the shot is heard Pearl twists and falls from the horse's back. The horse continues running away.

Mullison comes out of the wagon holding a bag of money.

Hygatt, to Mullison: "Nice Bunny. Now you're getting into the spirit of things."

The group turns and walks out of the area of the campsite toward their own horses.

◎

At dawn the sun begins to light the scene of terror and death. Hygatt's group has gone, taking Norton's wagon with them. Chuck's wagon, with the team of horses, stands where it was before. The bodies of Mr. and Mrs. Norton and Belger lie in the same positions as they were when killed.

Chuck's head is bloodstained. He comes to. He looks around him, struggles painfully to his feet, and staggers against the wagon. He looks around, taking in the three dead bodies and the debris of the Nortons' goods that Hygatt's men have left.

Chuck fights back to consciousness, and with a look of anguish on his face, turns and looks for Pearl. He sees her lying on the ground some distance off. She is unconscious and disheveled. Chuck kneels beside her and takes her head in his hands: "Pearl! Pearl!"

Her eyes open a moment, and then she turns her head away and sobs. Chuck holds her close to him and unable to control himself, he lowers his head, fighting back the sobs that well up inside of him. Then very slowly and carefully he lifts Pearl in his arms and starts for the wagon. He places the bloodstained figure in the wagon, harnesses the horses, pulls away from the scene of death, and heads back toward town.

◎

In front of the Sheriff's office are Chancel, Hellens, and Holly. The latter two are cinching the saddles of their horses. Chancel, who has just come down the steps of the office, carries two repeating rifles. He hands one of the rifles to Hellens, and then places the second rifle in his saddle holster. The three men are armed with six-shooters as well as rifles.

Saunders stands on the porch of his store, watching Chancel and the other men reflectively.

In front of the Black Jack saloon and in front of some of the other buildings stand some men who look idly at Chancel and the others.

Two men, Cubal and Brazer, are squatting, sitting on their heels. One of them chews on a little stick of wood.

Cubal: "First time I ever turned down ridin' with a posse."

Brazer: "The way I look at it—if 'Lysses ain't ridin' we shouldn't be ridin'."

A husband and wife stand watching. The woman's hand is on her husband's arm. "I'm glad you're not goin', Fred—glad."

The Man, a little angrily: "Stop talkin'." It is obvious that he is not quite as glad as his wife.

Saunders, on the porch, is still watching Chancel and the others. Then suddenly he straightens up and turns and walks into his store.

Hellens and Holly mount their horses. Chancel is about to mount his. He looks up at the two men.

Chancel: "There's only the three of us, and I don't know what we're goin' to head into. You can change your minds now, and I'll understand."

Holly: "Get on your horse, Wally, and let's start movin'."

Hellens, with a smile: "Speakin' for myself, Wally—I'm a terrible coward, but I just don't like the way things are goin'."

Wally smiles up at him, mounts his horse. Just then they hear the rapid sound of horses' hoofs and the rattling of a wagon. They look up.

Over the bridge from the east comes the wagon driven by Chuck. Everyone is sight turns his attention to the wagon, which tears into the end of the street and stops at the front of Saunders' store. The townspeople, knowing very well that something has happened, begin to group around the wagon. Chancel pushes through the people up to Chuck, who is just getting off the front of the wagon.

Chancel: "What's happened?"

Chuck: "Mr. and Mrs. Norton are dead, Belger's dead."

Chancel, gripping his hand: "Pearl?"

Chuck gives him a look and pushes him aside. He goes to the back of the wagon. He gets in and suddenly reappears. Crouching on his knee, he holds Pearl in his arms. She is unconscious. Chuck hands her over to Chancel. He jumps down from the wagon, and shaking his head "no" at Chancel he takes Pearl back in his arms. As he starts up the steps of Saunders' store, some of the others start with him.

Chuck, looking at them: "All of you wait here."

As the others drop back a little and watch, Chuck goes up the steps toward Saunders store carrying Pearl. His face is grim. The faces of the others who are watching are strained, anxious, tense. As Chuck reaches the doors, his foot kicks them open.

Saunders has been standing behind the counter watching, his hands flat on top of the counter, his face tight with fear. Chuck comes into the store carrying Pearl. Saunders looks at her, his hands going to her face. Gently Chuck places Pearl on the counter. With an unspoken question Saunders looks anxiously at Chuck.

Chuck, his voice low: "She's still alive, Mr. Saunders."

Saunders half-closes his eyes in pain.

Outside the store people are watching. Some of the men are looking at the wagon. Mrs. Chambers arrives and goes up the steps of Saunders' store.

She enters and goes over to where Chuck, Saunders, and Pearl are grouped. Chuck now turns to Mrs. Chambers: "I'll take her upstairs, Mrs. Chambers, and you and some of the women-folks can watch her."

He looks over at Saunders who slowly nods his head. Chuck takes Pearl in his arms again, and he and Mrs. Chambers walk out of the store. Saunders stands quietly a moment, and then over his face comes a look of determined and fierce rage. He walks over to the closet where he had previously placed his gun belt and revolver. Grimly he puts on his gun belt, ties the holster to his thigh; then he reaches into the closet again and brings out a Winchester repeating rifle. Again he digs into the closet and takes out a heavy bandolier of rifle bullets. He places that bandolier over his shoulders. He turns from the closet and slowly walks toward the front of the store.

Chuck and Mrs. Chambers have already disappeared up the stairway. The people look up as Saunders comes out on the porch of the store, his rifle gripped in his hands. He walks slowly and silently toward the people and down the steps to Chancel.

Saunders: "Hygatt killed three people." Then with a movement of his head: "You know about Pearl. I'm ridin' with you."

Suddenly there is a chorus of other voices. All the men there are calling out: "Me, too!" "I'm ridin' in." "We'll all ride."

They are now augmented by others joining the posse. Quist stands at the edge of the crowd. There is a chorus of voices: "What are we waitin' for?" "Me too!" "Let's get him." "Let's ride."

Saunders: "Swear us in, Wally!"

Chancel: "There ain't any regular oath." He looks at all the men, comes to a decision. "Raise your right hands."

All the men do, including Saunders. Chancel eyes them a moment.

Chancel, with a little nod: "You know what's gotta be done." A little pause: "All right, you're all sworn in." He then looks at Saunders. "Any suggestions, 'Lysses?"

Saunders: "We're gonna need every man we

can get. I think some of us ought to ride and bring in all the ranchers and all their hands."

Chancel nods.

Saunders: "First everybody come in and get your belts full and help yourselves to rifles."

He makes a gesture and starts up the steps, the crowd following him.

Quist does not enter the store. He moves away down the street, gets on his horse, and rides rapidly out of town. There is so much excitement around Saunders' store that no one pays any attention to Quist.

Saunders, in the store, is passing out large boxes of ammunition, which the men are breaking into. They load their belts. Then Saunders reaches to a long rack of rifles that he has had for sale. He hands out the rifles to the first hands that touch them. All the men are busy loading their belts, checking their guns. After a couple of moments the work is done. Chancel lifts his hands for attention: "Men!"

They quiet down.

Chancel: "Pass the word that we'll meet at the Pinon Canyon at midnight—that will give us enough time to reach Moon Creek at dawn."

Saunders: "Look, Wally. I got kind of an idea."

Wally looks at him and nods for Saunders to speak up.

Saunders: "They're gonna be over a hundred of us shootin' at a hundred of them—and it's gonna be hard to tell who's who."

Wally, with a nod: "Yeah?"

Saunders: "Most of us served in the war. Let's get any parts of our old uniforms—split 'em up—pants, jackets, hats. If anybody is wearin' part of a uniform—we'll know he's on our side."

Chancel nods. "You all heard that, men—let's get busy—Holly, you ride west to—"

The forces are gathering to fight Hygatt. Men ride up to small ranch houses, passing the word. Hands are grabbing rifles and saddling horses. Men are taking old uniforms out of closets. Two men divide a uniform between them, one fellow looking at the pants and the other fellow trying to get into the coat that is a little small for him. They laugh. The men have Union Civil War uniforms of every variety. Infantry jackets and short cavalry jackets and also zouave coats. There is even a double-breasted long naval coat.

That night a full moon lights Pinon Canyon with sharp, white highlights and deep, full shadows. In the Canyon are gathered most of the men who are to ride against Moon Creek. Others are riding up to join them. All are wearing some part of a uniform, most of them complete.

Saunders, in a cavalry officer's uniform, reveals the true fighting qualities that make him a dangerous man. Most of the men, now that they are wearing uniforms, take on a military aspect and bearing that they lose in civilian clothes. This is more than a posse. It is a group of well-trained, veteran soldiers prepared to go into battle. Chancel, in an infantry uniform, is standing in his stirrups, looking at the men grouped in back of him. He turns to Saunders: "I think most of 'em are here. The others can join us on the way."

Chuck, who wears a cavalry officer's coat: "Has Slavin come yet?"

Chancel shakes his head "no."

Saunders, looking over at Chuck: "The last time I rode in this uniform, Chuck, your father was ridin' next to me wearin' that coat." He puts his hand on Chuck's shoulder. "I'm glad there's a Slattery ridin' with me again."

Chuck nods. Chancel suddenly points toward

the mouth of the canyon. Coming in from that direction are a group of seven horsemen. One of the riders carries a cavalry guidon. It is Slavin and six of his sons. They are mounted and well-armed, and Slavin wears a Confederate officer's uniform. His sons between them wear different parts of the other branches of Confederate services.

Slavin and the boys ride up and pull to a stop. Slavin salutes in military fashion. Saunders returns it. This is done very deliberately.

Slavin: "Just after we got word, some of Hygatt's men raided us. I lost one of my boys. The youngest."

Saunders: "We've all got a lot of scores to settle for, Slavin—Captain Slavin."

Slavin: "Three of my boys fought in the war, and there was enough uniforms to go 'round. I brought my old battle guidon and a bugle."

Saunders: "We may want that bugle. Have your boys ride next to you."

Slavin nods.

Chancel, looking at a watch: "We better move, 'Lysses."

Saunders nods. Chancel rises in his stirrups, lifts his hand, looks back at the men, and makes a gesture of "Forward."

There is the rustle of men settling into saddles, and as the entire group starts toward the mouth of the canyon, there is the muffled sound of over a hundred horses moving.

From out of the mouth of the canyon into the bright moonlight come the riders. There is the creak of leather and the sound of horses. Men, more men, and more come out and up on the plain.

Slavin's attention is attracted to something. He reaches over and taps Saunders, who looks. Chancel's attention has now been drawn, and he suddenly lifts his hand and rises in his stirrups again, signalling the men to stop.

Coming toward them are three horses. On these horses ride Mrs. Franson, Mr. Franson, and in the center Quist, whose hands are tied. His horse is led by Mrs. Franson, who is wearing the hat "direct from Paris, France" that she bought from Wesley Perkins. Mr. Franson, his face drawn, sits his horse, leaning heavily on the pommel. Quist, frightened and worried, eyes them all, panic-stricken.

Several men speak at once:

"The Fransons."

"What's Quist doing with him?"

"It's Mr. and Mrs. Franson."

"What's the matter with Jack?"

Chuck: "Are you all right, Jack?"

Mrs. Franson: "I can talk to you now, Chuck. They killed Poling and put a knife in Jack's back. They threatened to kill me and Jack if I talked. Quist came the place late this afternoon and warned them about the posse. They're all gathering in Moon Creek waitin' for you."

Franson: "Quist tipped 'em off beforehand about Norton's ridin' with the money."

Mrs. Franson: "He's been paid right along to spy and help murder his neighbors."

Chancel, grimly: "Anything to say, Quist?"

Quist shakes his head.

Franson: "When Gribbles and the rest of 'em took off for Moon Creek, they left Quist to keep an eye on us." He looks at Quist with a hard smile, then looks back at Saunders. "But he didn't have an eye in the back of his head when Anna hit him with a flat iron."

Chuck: "We got a four-hour ride. Let's string him up and get goin'."

Quist sits silently shaking his head but unable to utter a sound.

Chancel, looking over at Saunders and Slavin: "Do we all agree that it's a hangin' offense?"

Saunders, slowly: "Betrayin' your own folks—is worse than murder." He nods his head. "String him up."

Slowly Slavin also nods his head.

Chancel looks around in the direction of the other men grouped close by. They all nod silently. Quist remains seated on his horse, just shaking his head. Chancel moves his horse toward Quist.

Chancel again rises in his stirrups, makes a gesture of "Forward!" The column moves on, the men looking up at Quist's body as they pass. The men's interest in looking is merely one of casual curiosity and contempt.

They ride out on the moonlit prairie headed toward Moon Creek.

◎

Just before dawn in Moon Creek the town seems unoccupied, but preparations have been made for an attack. A short barricade has been erected at the end of the street, and in front of this barricade a ditch has been dug. The barricade, which consists of wagons put end to end and with barrels and other odds and ends packed under them, is well fortified, with men, who motionless, wait for the attack. The windows of the houses are all guarded by more men with rifles and shotguns. The porches of the building and the roofs of the porches are also peopled with motionless men who wait.

At the offices of the Two Axes Mining Company are Hygatt, Mullison, Gerrett, Gribbles, and Yunker. Hygatt, in the manner of a general inspecting his defenses, struts about, his eyes taking in all the features of the defense system. He turns to Mullison: "We're ready to receive our friends."

Mullison, a little shaken: "I don't feel like makin' jokes, Hygatt. I know what these men do when they get in action. You won't find them easy like Gorman and Poling."

Hygatt, looking at Gerrett: "You ought to explain to Mr. Mullison that you can't make a profit without taking a risk."

Suddenly a man shouts: "Take a look, Mr. Hygatt."

Hygatt looks up in the direction of the voice, coming from a man on the roof of a porch. He is holding a gun, and his right hand indicates the direction he is looking off at. Hygatt and the others walk up the two steps leading up to the porch and look out in the direction indicated.

The dawn is just coming up across the plains east of Moon Creek. A morning cloud of mist combined with dust creates the illusion of a feathery cloud of smoke. Out of this cloud, with the rising sun back of them, comes the troop of ranchers from Homeville. With this backlighting and with the cloud effect, nothing can be seen distinctly. It is rather hazy and soft-looking, almost dreamlike, and the riders look like strange, crusading figures coming out of the sky, a vision of warrior angels. This effect is increased by the fact that the men are still not galloping their horses. They are walking them slowly, deliberately. In the vanguard ride Saunders, Slavin, Chuck, Chancel, and the Fransons.

Hygatt steps down from the porch and calls out to his men: "They don't seem in much of a hurry, boys—looks like they're scared even before the shootin' starts."

Mullison, nervously: "They got some kind of scheme, Hygatt. I'm tellin' ya!"

Hygatt, furiously: "Shut up. They'll never get into Moon Creek."

◎

The body of riders still walk their horses slowly, evenly, determinedly. They look not like a normal sheriff's posse, but like veteran cavalry.

Franson: "I'm itchin' to go."

Saunders: "Save the horses till we get within gunshot."

They continue their slow, even walk.

There is an air of nervousness about Hygatt's men at the barricade. Mullison stands nearby with Hygatt.

Hygatt, looking out toward the plains: "They make a very pretty picture." Then to his men: "Fire a few rounds at 'em. That'll change their minds."

Some of Hygatt's men begin firing.

The troop of riders still walk slowly. Many yards in front of them the bullets fired by Hygatt's men kick up little spurts of dust. The men are still not within range. The firing continues, but the men move slowly as before.

◉

Yunker: "You're wastin' lead, Hygatt. Let 'em come a little closer."

Hygatt, beginning to feel a little tension: "I'm givin' the orders, Yunker. Don't try to tell me what to do." Then looking at the other men: "Keep firing, I tell you!"

Mullison: "We ought to get out of here." Nervously: "We haven't got a chance."

Hygatt, looking at Mullison: "No one's stopping you. Run if you want to."

Mullison, panic-stricken: "I'm going."

He runs off, Hygatt watching him. Mullison jumps on his horse and spurs him. Hygatt is looking at Mullison. He levels his revolver and fires three times in rapid succession. Mullison's body stiffens as the bullets hit him. His body slides slowly off the horse, and the horse, continuing running, drags Mullison through the dust as his boot is caught in one of the stirrups.

Hygatt watches Mullison for a minute, then turns to Yunker: "I always give them an even chance of running away." He turns and starts shooting out toward the Chancel and Saunders troop.

Spurts of dust come closer to the troop of riders. Suddenly one of the horses is hit. As the horse sinks to his knees, the rider jumps off and onto the back of another horse. At that moment Saunders nods to Chancel.

Chancel, calling out to Slavin's boy: "Blow the charge, son!"

Slavin's boy lifts the bugle and as he blows the charge, Chuck and Saunders gesture the group on. There is an answering chorus of yells and screams. Slavin's boys give a rebel yell, and the whole troop breaks into a furious gallop. As they start, they fire their guns.

The fire is returned by the Moon Creek defenders.

The troop rides, spread out now, galloping furiously toward Moon Creek. They are in a single line, and they are shooting. One of the men falls.

As the firing continues, one of the men stationed on a roof in Moon Creek is hit and falls to the ground.

The first group of riders reaches Moon Creek. They vault their horses over the shallow ditch and over the barricade, shooting as they go. One or two of the horses are hit, but the first defense line has been broken and the riders swarm into the town.

There is tight action in crowded rooms where Moon Creek defenders go for the last stand. A few defenders are jammed together in the mine pit, where they are sought out and finished off by the attackers. A Moon Creek ruffian attempts to light cases of dynamite but is cut down by Chuck, who then hands out sticks of dynamite to the attackers, and they employ them in blowing up and igniting some of the buildings in Moon Creek. Men are shot from horses; men fall from the roofs. Cavalry sabers are used to cut down some of Hygatt's mob. Chancel, Saunders, Franson, and Chuck are all fighting furiously. As the struggle nears its end, Chancel is wounded in the shoulder, but as he falls he kills Gerrett, who pitches headlong into a flaming building.

Gribbles kills Mrs. Franson but is trapped by

Mr. Franson who jumps him and knifes Gribbles to death. It is Slavin and two of his sons who corner Al Yunker and two or three of Yunker's men and massacre the bunch of them. Chuck and Saunders trap Hygatt in the office of the Two Axes Mining Company and as Hygatt wounds Chuck slightly in one hand, Saunders and Chuck pour bullets from their six-shooters into Hygatt who spins around crazily and falls dead at their feet. As the remainder of Hygatt's mob surrenders, the village of Moon Creek is partially in flames. Saunders remarks laconically, "Let it burn," and the Homeville troop corrals the survivors of Hygatt's gang and starts to move out into the prairie.

Three or four hours later the remains of Moon Creek are still smoking and burning. Nearby are Slavin, Chancel (his shoulder bandaged), Saunders, Chuck, and Franson. Graves have been dug, and the group of riders, some mounted on their horses, others standing, are near the graves. A good number of the men have crude bandages around their hands or heads. They are tired and spent.

Chancel, facing the graves, takes off his hat. Saunders removes his, and as he does this all the other men remove theirs.

Chancel, looking at the graves: "May the good Lord in His mercy rest the souls of these men."

There is a chorus of mumbled "Amens." Chancel looks up and around at the other men.

There is another pause and then Chancel puts on his hat. The others do the same and mount their horses.

The troop has now started back toward Homeville. They are moving along, Hygatt's men bunched in the center, guarded by them. The head of the column reaches a rise in the prairie. They move up the rise and down the other side, disappearing from view. On the top of the rise sit Saunders, Chancel, Slavin, Chuck, and Franson. They are looking back in the direction of Moon Creek from which eddies of smoke are rising.

Chancel, sadly: "Once again good men are buried in ground that they died to keep free."

Saunders, slowly: "Maybe this time we've learned a bit. Hygatt and everything he stood for could have been destroyed without all this killing if we had gotten together earlier. I'm as much to blame as anybody. But maybe now we'll all work together believin' that if evil happens to our neighbor—it happens to us."

Chancel and the others nod. They look back reflectively at Moon Creek a moment and then turning their horses from the scene of destruction and violence they move on, disappearing down the other side of the knoll and across the prairie.

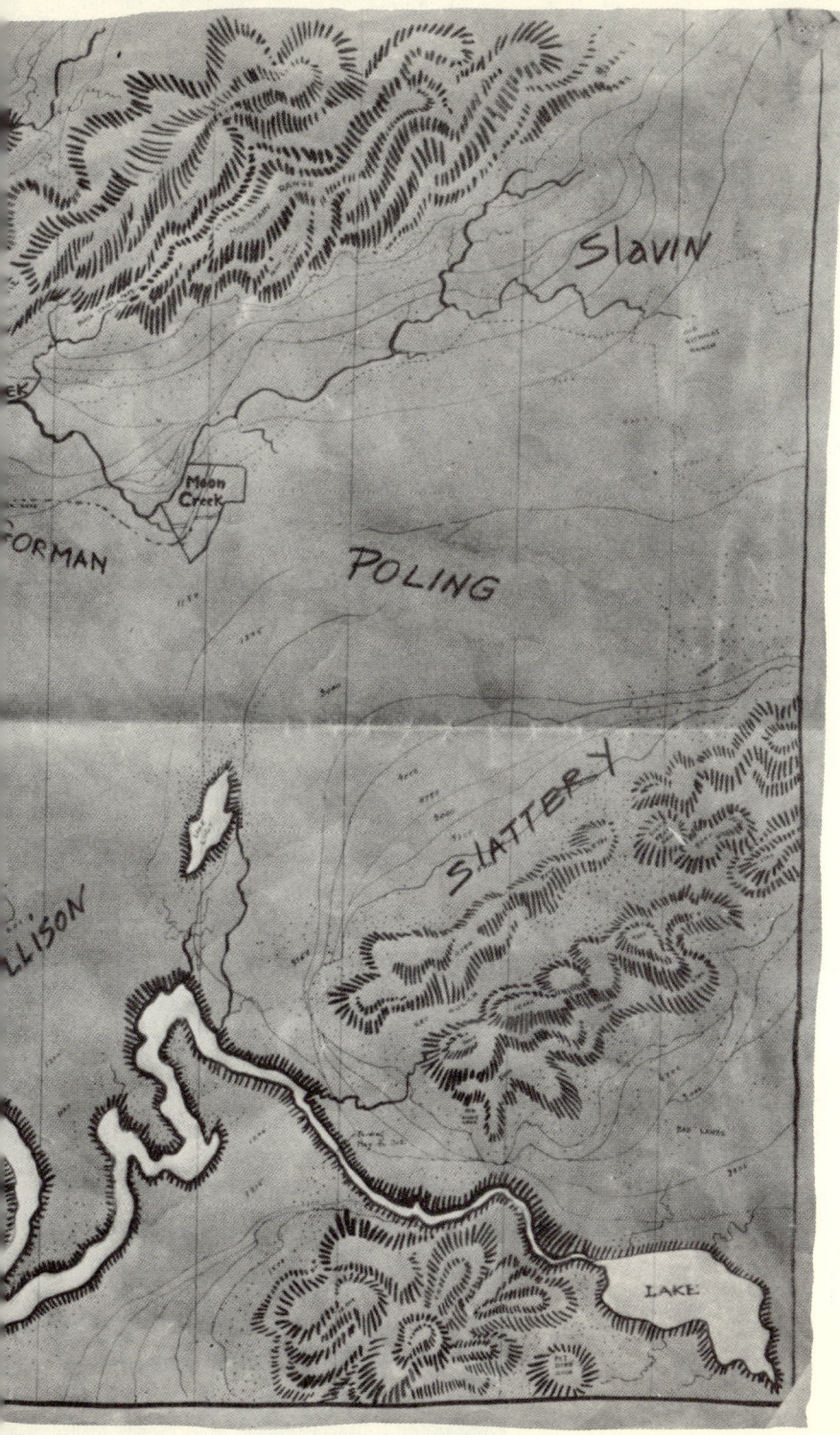